HARDSCRABBLE

# Hardscrabble

by

SANDRA DALLAS

PUBLISHED *by* SLEEPING BEAR PRESS

Text copyright © 2018 Sandra Dallas
Cover illustration © 2018 by Steve Adams

## Sleeping Bear Press™

2395 South Huron Parkway, Suite 200, Ann Arbor, MI 48104
www.sleepingbearpress.com
© Sleeping Bear Press

Printed and bound in the United States.
Library of Congress Cataloging-in-Publication Data
Names: Dallas, Sandra, author.
Title: Hardscrabble / written by Sandra Dallas.
Description: Ann Arbor, MI : Sleeping Bear Press, [2018] | Summary:
Twelve-year-old Belle Martin and her family move to Mingo, Colorado, in
1910 when the U.S. government offers 320 acres of land free to homesteaders.
Identifiers: LCCN 2017029809
ISBN 9781585363759 (hc) 10 9 8 7 6 5 4 3 2
ISBN 9781585363766 (pbk) 10 9 8 7 6 5 4 3 2 1
Subjects: | CYAC: Frontier and pioneer life—Colorado—Fiction. | Family
life—Colorado—Fiction. | Neighbors—Fiction.
Colorado—History—1876-1950—Fiction.
Classification: LCC PZ7.D1644 Har 2018 | DDC [Fic]—dc23
LC record available at https://lccn.loc.gov/2017029809

*For Forrest and his cousin, the amazing Magnolia Marie Cole.*

CHAPTER ONE

# Coming to Colorado

e o

"Where's Papa?" Belle Martin asked, looking around the train station.

Carrie shook her head. "Hush," she whispered.

Belle frowned. Was Carrie suggesting that if she hadn't asked about Papa, Mama wouldn't have noticed he wasn't there to meet them?

Belle searched the depot, hoping to spot her father. Perhaps he was lost in the crowd of people milling about. She saw men removing farm equipment that had come in on the train and putting it into wagons. A boy helped his father lift bags of seeds out of one of the cars and stack them on the depot platform. A woman wearing a worn shawl over her head tried to hold on to half a dozen children, talking to them in a language Belle didn't understand. Carrie had told her they were immigrants, people who had come to America from other countries hoping for a better life. They expected to farm in Colorado. Women got off the train and stood on the metal platform and searched the crowd for their husbands, then smiled when they found them.

Belle watched one woman as she hugged a man. As his face turned red, he removed her arms. But she would have none of it. "Six months since I've seen you, and I've the right to a little affection," she said.

But there was no Papa.

One by one, as their husbands claimed them, the women left the platform, a few getting into automobiles or trucks but most into wagons. The immigrants, too, crowded into rickety wagons and drove off across the brown prairie, leaving only the Martins. A few people glanced at Mama, who looked frail and sick and leaned against Carrie for support. But they didn't ask what was wrong or offer to help. And nobody paid attention to Belle, who stood at the edge of the rough boards, holding the hands of two little girls, Sarah, age four, and Becky, two. Belle's brother Frank, eleven, sat on one of their trunks with another brother, Gully, five. Beside them were boxes and barrels of dishes and pots and pans and sacks of flour and sugar. There were containers of salt and spices and dozens of other items Mama thought they would need on a farm.

"We haven't seen Papa for six months, either. Where is he, Belle? Is he coming?" Frank asked.

"He'll be here. He expects us. He promised to meet us." Then she added, "Maybe he got the day wrong. This is June 11, 1910, isn't it? And this is Mingo, Colorado, isn't it?"

Frank shrugged in a *How would I know?* gesture.

Belle tried not to think of the conversation she had overheard on the train. A man had been talking about a woman who had arrived in Mingo just a week earlier to meet her husband, only to discover he wasn't there at all. He was supposed to have left the East to file for a homestead near Mingo, but instead he'd taken their money and run off. So there she was, no husband and not enough money to buy a ticket back to where she'd come from. Belle half expected to see the woman standing on the platform still, but, of course, she was gone.

The Martins, too, didn't have the money for return

tickets to Iowa. That was why they had come here, because their money was gone. But she wasn't worried. Papa wasn't like that man. He loved them. He'd written home that he was counting the days until his family joined him.

She glanced at her big sister. Carrie was fifteen, three years older than Belle, four years older than Frank. Carrie held tight to Mama, who was holding the baby in her arms. The baby was only six weeks old and didn't have a name. Mama had said she'd wait until they got to Colorado so that Papa could name him.

Mama had felt poorly even before the baby came. The doctor had told her she was not to go to Colorado until he was born. Then after the baby arrived, the doctor had wanted her to stay in Iowa for a few more months before moving to Mingo. She still wasn't well. But Mama had insisted she would be fine as soon as she saw Papa. The sight of him would be better than any rest—or medicine, either, she'd claimed.

Mama didn't seem worried that Papa hadn't met them, but Belle could tell that Carrie was. Carrie led Mama to a bench and told her to rest. Mama nodded and sat down, the baby in her lap. Then Carrie went to Belle. She'd forgotten she'd told Belle to hush, and she whispered, "I don't understand where Papa is. He ought to be here. It's not right, his making Mama wait."

"He's coming," Belle said. "You always worry." She was right. Sometimes, Carrie acted like a grown-up. She fussed over Mama, and she often did the cooking and washing and caring for the baby when Mama was tired.

"He'll be here," Belle said stubbornly. She looked out across the prairie. The grasses, gold in the late-afternoon sun, waved in the wind that blew dust and dirt onto the platform. There wasn't a tree to block the view. There wasn't a sign of Papa, either.

"I don't think Mingo's what Mama expected it to be," Carrie said. "She told me there'd be crops and flowers, that it would be green. I've never seen so much brown. It's ugly." Carrie glanced at her mother, who sat softly humming to the baby.

Belle stared at her sister for a moment. Although she sometimes brooded, Carrie, like their mother, rarely complained. When trouble came, Carrie would press her lips together, then smile and say that things could be worse. "Well," she said, smiling now at Belle, "I think this farm will be a fine one, different from Iowa. Papa's a good farmer, and it looks like he won't have to cut down trees." She gave a laugh. "We won't have a mortgage, either." Still, she said, "I hope the house Papa built for us will be better than the dirt huts and tar-paper shacks we saw along the train tracks. I wouldn't want Mama to live in something like that."

Belle agreed. They had had a nice home in Iowa, a brick house with white jigsaw trim hanging from the roof. The house was big, with four bedrooms, and there was running water in the kitchen. And an indoor bathroom. But the crops had failed over the last three years, and the bank took away the farm. And then Mama was sick long before the baby came. The doctor said she needed a change of climate. He told Papa to take her west, where the air was clear and dry. So Papa decided to try his hand at homesteading. The government promised to give a man 320 acres of land for free. All he had to do was live on it for five years and farm it. That sounded like a fine opportunity. So Papa set off for Mingo to file for a homestead, leaving his family to follow later.

Belle looked out across the high plains once more. She believed she could almost see the earth curve. She'd learned at school that the earth was a giant ball. *A dusty ball in*

*Colorado*, she thought as she watched far off on the horizon as tumbleweeds rolled across the plains. The conductor on the train had pointed out the weeds to them, saying they were Russian thistles but everybody called them tumbleweeds because of the way the wind sent them tumbling across the fields. She stared in that direction for a long time, and then she grabbed Frank's arm, excited. "Look. I think that's a wagon."

"Papa?" Carrie said. She went to Mama and took her arm. "See over there, a wagon. It *has* to be Papa. We knew he'd come."

"Of course we did," Mama replied, looking around her as if she hadn't realized her children were worried. "I never doubted it for a minute."

The wagon moved quickly across the open ground, and in a few minutes, it was at the depot. Papa jumped out and landed on the platform with a bound. He grabbed Mama in his arms and hugged her. "I'd been here sooner, but the wheel on the wagon broke just as I was leaving. I had to go to the neighbor's to borrow this wagon."

"We knew there was a reason," Mama said, beaming at him. "But what does it matter? Now you're here, Beck."

Papa hugged her again, then turned to the others. "Carrie, what would your mother have done without you? And my little Bluebelle, sassy as ever." He hugged both of his older daughters, then shook hands with Frank, telling him he was glad there was another man now to help with the farm. He shook hands with Gully, too. Then he picked up Sarah and Becky, one girl in each arm and said they'd grown so much, he wouldn't have known them. "Why, last time I saw you, Becky, you couldn't even walk."

Becky stared and then asked, "Are you Papa?"

"Of course I am! I'll never stay away from you this long again."

At last, he went back to Mama and peered down at the baby. "Why, who's this button here? I believe you've added another little Martin to our family. He certainly seems to be a Martin. Just look at those ears." The baby's ears stuck out just like Papa's and Frank's. "What do you call him?"

"Baby," Carrie put in. "Mama says you're to name him. Just like you did all of us."

Papa nodded. He had named Carrie and Frank after his parents. Belle was supposed to be named for Mama's mother, but when he saw her bright blue eyes, Papa had said they were the color of bluebells. So he'd called her Bluebelle. Sarah and Gully were named after Mama's folks and Becky after himself. "What name do you favor for this little one, Louisa?" he asked Mama.

"He should be called something for our new home. But I don't see any bluebells out here," Mama replied.

"There's buffalo grass, but that's not much of a name for a boy." Papa thought a moment, and then he reached for the baby, who was so small that Papa could hold him in one hand. He peeled back the blanket and grinned at the infant. "What name would you like, young sir? What would you think of Louis? It's a good deal like your mother's name." He glanced over at Mama. "What do you think of it, Louisa?"

"I never favored it," Mama told him. "He ought to have a western name, a Colorado name."

Papa looked out across the prairie, then turned to us and grinned. "What do you say to Sagebrush?" he asked. "First name will be Louis and middle name Sagebrush. We'll call him Sage."

"Sage," Mama repeated. "I think that's a fine name." She took back the baby and told Papa, "Now, it's time to take Sage to his new home. We're all of us tired out."

Papa, Frank, and Belle loaded the trunks and bags and boxes of foodstuffs into the wagon. Then Papa lifted Mama and the baby onto the board seat. The rest of the family climbed into the wagon bed, and they started out across the prairie. As the depot disappeared behind them, Frank said, "I like this place. I could ride a horse a hundred miles out here. Do you think Papa will let me ride one of the horses, Belle?"

"I do. I think he'll let me ride, too—astride. And I'll be able to run footraces and wear short skirts and not have to worry about what people will think, because there won't be anybody to see me," she said. "Don't you think Colorado's swell, Carrie?"

Carrie had seated herself on one of the trunks, and she, too, stared out at the land. There was a look of shock on her face, and Belle wondered what her sister thought of the prairie. Like Mama, however, she would never complain. She would make the best of things.

"Why, I like it fine," she replied.

# The Girl Homesteader

The train had arrived at noon. It was midafternoon by the time Papa had loaded the wagon and driven the three miles from Mingo to the homestead. He stopped the wagon next to a strange building that looked like it had been carved out of the prairie. "This is your new home. Isn't it a dinger?" he said. There was a touch of pride in his voice.

"It's dirt," Carrie blurted out, and then she bit her lip. "I mean, it looks just like it's made out of grass."

"Right you are," Papa said. "It's made of layers of sod. That's why it's called a soddy. I wrote you about it."

"I didn't know it looked like this," Carrie said. "Did you, Mama?"

"It's a fine house," Mama said.

"Of course it is," Carrie said quickly. "It's just that I'm surprised."

"I made it myself. Well, mostly by myself. Some of the neighbors helped. One loaned me his sod plow. You use it to break the sod, which is the prairie earth covered with buffalo grass. Then you cut it into strips. The strips are eighteen inches long and twelve inches wide." He turned to Carrie when he said that, since she loved math.

"Sod breaking is hard work, because the buffalo grass is tough. Sometimes I think the roots go all the way to China. A neighbor helped me load the strips onto a low sledge and haul them over here. Then I stacked them one on top of another to form walls. Our house is seven feet high," he said.

"Won't the sod slip?" Belle asked.

"The roots of each layer cling to the sod strip beneath it. These walls are so thick, they keep out the wind. A soddy is the best kind of house out here, much better than frame. It's warm in winter and cool in summer. Look, I even put in a glass window. And a wooden door. Some people hang blankets in the doorways, but I wanted a nice, tight house for my family. I plan to put in a board floor one day."

"It's a splendid house, Beck," Mama said.

"It's a dinger, all right," Frank said. He liked Papa's new word.

Belle went up close to the house, poking a finger between two layers of sod. Then she said, "Look, there are flowers growing out of the walls. I like it already."

Becky pointed at the flowers growing on the roof and began to laugh.

"What do you think, Carrie?" Papa asked.

Carrie was silent for a minute, and then she laughed, too. "Mama and I won't have to sweep dirt off the floor, because the floor is dirt."

When the others started for the house, Belle whispered to her sister, "Is that what's meant by dirt-poor?"

"No, of course not. Don't forget we have the money Aunt Susan left for me to go to college."

"So we're not poor?"

"Not poor at all," Carrie insisted, turning to look at the family. "How could we be when we have each other? It's just that we don't have money."

ℓℓℓ

Papa led them inside their new home, which was the strangest house any of them had ever seen. The inside walls were rough and grassy just like those on the outside. The house had just two rooms. The larger was the kitchen. Papa had fastened shelves to one wall, and near it stood a two-burner cookstove. A table he had made was in the center of the room, surrounded by half a dozen nail kegs and apple boxes serving as stools. There was no bureau, just one cupboard. There weren't curtains, a rug, or a tablecloth, either. The smaller room held an iron bed. Belle looked at the dirt floor and knew that the big crocheted rug Mama had made for the bedroom would stay in the trunk.

"Look, Louisa. I made a bed for Sage," Papa said, pointing to a wooden box on runners.

"A cradle! You made a cradle for Sage to sleep in," Mama said.

"But where are the rest of us going to sleep?" Frank asked.

"On the floor in the big room. We'll cover the dirt with a tarp so your quilts won't get dirty."

"It will be just like camping," Carrie said and smiled at him.

Belle thought that was an odd remark, because her sister didn't like to camp.

"When you're settled, I'll build bunk beds," Papa said. "What with putting in the crops and building the house, I didn't have time." He looked at Mama, and for the first time, there was doubt on his face.

"Of course you didn't," Mama said, smiling at him. She sat down on one of the apple boxes and unwrapped baby Sage.

"Why don't you stay there, Mama? I'll fix you a cup of coffee," Carrie said.

Papa took down a can of coffee from the shelf and said, "The brand is Arbuckle's. It's called the coffee that won the west. All the homesteaders drink it."

Carrie looked around and spotted the kindling bucket next to the stove. "Where's the pump, Papa? I didn't see it."

"There isn't one. The water barrel's outside. We have to haul water from the river half a mile away."

"I'll fill the pail," Belle offered. While Carrie built a fire in the stove, then ground the coffee, Belle picked up a bucket and went to the barrel for water. Papa and Frank began unloading the wagon.

"I'll make coffee for all of us," Carrie said.

"For me, too?" Belle asked.

Carrie smiled at her. "I don't see why not. You're a homesteader now."

*℮℮*

"Hello, the house," a voice called from outside.

Sage was asleep in his cradle, and Gully, Sarah, and Becky were playing on the floor, tin cups of water beside them. The rest of the Martins were sitting around the make-shift table, drinking coffee. Belle made a brave attempt to swallow her coffee, but although it made her feel grown-up to drink it, she didn't like it. She had doctored it twice with evaporated milk from a can Carrie had pried open. They all looked up when they heard the voice.

"That'll be Lizzie Cord," Papa said. "She's our closest neighbor. She lives a quarter mile away. Lizzie's a homesteader."

"With her husband, of course," Mama said.

"No, she's a bachelor girl. There are one or two other girl homesteaders on the other side of Mingo."

"Think of that!" Mama said. She and Carrie exchanged a look. "Miss Cord must be a strong-willed woman," Mama said.

"I bet she's built like a horse," Carrie observed. Then realizing that wasn't a nice thing to say, she added, "I mean, she must be as strong as a horse."

Belle pictured the girl homesteader as a large woman, probably as big as a man. She wondered if she would be dressed in overalls with a felt hat and would maybe even be smoking a pipe.

"Come on in and meet the family, Lizzie," Papa called, standing up. Carrie stood too, and went to the stove for the coffeepot, then looked around for a cup. But there weren't any more cups. She quickly finished her own coffee, then wiped out her cup and filled it for the newcomer. Belle wished she'd thought of doing that, so that she wouldn't have to finish the foul-tasting brew. *A girl homesteader as strong as a horse would like coffee*, she thought.

They all turned to the door and stared as a young woman no bigger than Carrie entered the soddy. She wore a stylish black skirt and a starched shirtwaist. Belle's mouth dropped open. *That* was a girl homesteader? Lizzie's pretty

17

hair curled around her face, and she wore a smart little hat with a feather.

"Well, hello!" she burst out. "I've been almost as excited as Beck that you were coming. Imagine having women neighbors almost at my doorstep. Welcome to Colorado." She went to Mama and pumped her hand. "I am very glad to meet you at last."

"Thank you, Miss Cord," Mama said.

"Elizabeth will do, or Lizzie if you like. Let's not stand on ceremony," she said. "I call your mister Beck, and I'll call you Louisa if you'll let me. Or is it Lou?"

"Louisa," Mama said. She didn't like being called Lou.

"And you must be Carrie. And Bluebelle," Lizzie continued, going from one to another, singing out names.

Carrie handed Lizzie the coffee, and the young woman said, "Why, bless your heart. You've only arrived, and here you are handing out refreshments." She took the coffee and gulped it down.

"Will you sit?" Carrie asked, pointing to the apple box she herself had been sitting on.

Lizzie shook her head. "Last thing you want is company. I just came by with your supper. It isn't much, but we get by without too much out here. It's beans with a bit of fatback, potatoes, some lettuce from my garden. There's a dried-apple cake, too."

"I *love* dried apples," Frank said.

"That's good, but you'll get mighty tired of them before too long." Then she added, "I put a bit of sourdough starter in there, as yeast is tricky out here. Just store it in a cool place and add a cup or two to your bread dough. Then add water and flour to feed the starter. There's women out here who've had their starter for years."

"We can't thank you enough. Carrie and I haven't given a thought to supper—or to bread making." Mama had risen when Lizzie came into the house, and now she sat down and pointed to Carrie's apple box. "We'd be pleased if you'd join us, even for a minute."

"You do that," Papa said. "I'll get the box of supper out of your wagon."

"It's your wagon. I fixed your wheel. Thought you'd be too busy, what with settling your family and all."

"Fixed it?" Carrie asked. "*You* fixed the wheel?"

Lizzie laughed. "When you're a woman by yourself out here, you learn to do a lot of things."

"How can you homestead by yourself? You're a girl," Carrie said.

Lizzie smiled at her. "It sounds a little scary, doesn't it? It was at first, of course, but it's not now. I wouldn't want to be anyplace else. It's a hardscrabble life, but I love it. You see, I always wanted to have a home of my very own, but I couldn't afford to buy one. I was a teacher before I came here, and I wasn't paid very much."

"So was Mama," Carrie told her. "And I'm going to be one, too. I'm going to teachers college when I graduate from high school. I'm going back to Iowa to live with my grandmother. The money's all been put aside."

"I couldn't stand to be cooped up indoors. I guess I'm a wild thing." Lizzie looked around the table and stopped at Belle. "Like you. You've a wild spirit, too. At least, that's what your papa tells me. You'll like running around the prairie more than sitting in a schoolroom."

Belle grinned. She would indeed like homesteading. She hoped that Carrie would, too.

As if Lizzie knew what Belle was thinking, she turned to Carrie. "It takes time. At first, you think the plains are frightening. But you'll come to love them. The sky is big and open. The whole world seems to be outside your door. You can breathe here. And the grass, when the late-day sun shines on it, shimmers like gold. There's joy in stripping off this old buffalo grass and turning the earth into farmland. *Your* farmland. Why, I went back home to Chicago once and couldn't stand to be cooped up on those dark streets with all the dirty buildings. I couldn't wait to get back to my prairie. The land grows on you."

"How can you farm by yourself?" Mama asked. "Does Beck help you?"

Papa came into the room, carrying a wooden box that smelled of good things to eat. He laughed. "It's the other way around. Lizzie helped *me*," he said. "I thought I was a pretty good farmer when I came here. But I didn't know a thing about dryland farming. Lizzie taught me."

Lizzie looked embarrassed. "We help each other out here. The Rileys on the next farm over taught me."

Papa winked at her. "Especially Joe Riley. He's one of the young men around Mingo who've taken a shine to our Lizzie here. She may not be an independent woman for long."

Lizzie shook her head. "You tease me all you want, Beck, but I'm not so anxious for a husband that I'd take just anybody. And Joe Riley is just anybody. I'd want someone who suits me. So I may never marry. I like my life just fine the way it is."

She stood and said she had overstayed her welcome. "We depend on each other out here. So you ask if you need anything. I've got washtubs and a scrub board and pots and pans. And I have a sewing machine."

"A sewing machine!" Carrie said. They hadn't had one even in Iowa.

Lizzie started for the door, but just then, a clod of dirt dropped from the ceiling onto her hat. She took off the hat and threw the dirt out the door. "You might want to tack muslin to the ceiling to keep the dirt from falling on you." She gave Papa a sideways glance. "You see, there are things women homesteaders know that men don't."

# *Visitors*

∽

The next morning, Mama and Carrie tackled the cleaning and organizing of the soddy. Papa told Belle to help them, but Carrie shook her head. "I know you'd rather be outdoors. Mama and I will clean the house and take care of the little ones. You go on with Papa. You'll be a great help to him."

"Really?" Belle asked. "I'll stay if you want me to." *Please say no*, she thought. *Please.*

"There's not room for the three of us in this kitchen. We'd just get in each other's way," Carrie told her.

Belle knew her sister was being kind. The house was made of dirt, and it was dirty. Clods of dirt had fallen from the ceiling. The glass window was so stained, they could barely see out. The dishes had to be unpacked and the food-stuffs put away. There were the breakfast dishes to be washed and dinner to prepare and maybe the washing, since Papa had left a heap of dirty clothes in the small room. Sage's diapers had to be washed too, and someone had to look after the three little ones. Mama would do what she could, but most of the work would fall on Carrie.

"When you're finished, Carrie, I'll drive us around the fields so you can see what I've done," Papa promised. "I've planted wheat, barley, and oats. Mama and the others will want to see it, too."

Carrie gave Belle a look that said, *When we're done?* Carrie and Mama never would be done.

Belle helped Carrie for a time. She washed the dishes and began unpacking boxes, but she kept bumping into her mother and sister. So Carrie told her to run along. Outside, Belle, her arms out as if she were flying in the wind, hurried to the crude barn. June, the cow, and the two horses were stabled there. "Will you let me ride one of the horses, Papa? Frank, too?"

Papa shook his head. "There's work for you to do, too, Belle. Later on, you can help with the fields, but right now your job is to take care of the kitchen garden. I didn't plant much, just potatoes and beets, carrots, turnips, cabbage. Next year we'll put in pumpkins and squash and lettuce. I haven't had time to hoe, and the weeds are thick. You'll have to do the weeding and pick off the potato bugs." Belle made a face. She hated the thick, slimy potato bugs.

"Maybe Gully can help. Sarah, too," Papa added.

Hearing their names, the two younger children ran to Belle. "I want to help," Gully said.

"Me too," Sarah told her sister.

Belle sighed. They would be more trouble than help. Still, Carrie didn't need to have them underfoot in the house. Then an idea struck her. "I know. You can pick off the potato bugs. Go ask Carrie if there's a lard pail—two lard pails. It will be a contest to see who can get the most bugs." The two ran back into the house for the pails, and Belle smiled to herself. A contest would not only encourage her brother and sister to take on the hated task of picking off potato bugs but also keep them occupied all morning.

ℓℓℓ

They had almost finished dinner and were getting up to start the afternoon chores when they heard a motorcar come down the dirt road and pull to a stop beside the soddy. "More neighbors," Papa said.

"Coming to check us out, no doubt. I'm afraid we won't make much of a first impression," Mama said. "If my good dress weren't at the bottom of the trunk, I'd put it on."

"That doesn't matter out here. You'll find folks don't get ragged out the way they do in the city."

"Now, what would you know about that, Beck?" Mama asked as she caught a glimpse of a woman wearing a driving costume and a hat with a veil, stepping down from the automobile. It was a big touring car with pull-down shades in the side windows. The woman was tall, her white hair pulled back in a fashionable twist. Mama touched her own dark brown hair, which was knotted at the back of her neck, and as she stood, she smoothed out her skirt. Mama was a pretty woman, small and slim—*too slim*, Belle thought, because she had lost weight after baby Sage was born. Carrie looked a good deal like her, although Carrie was taller, her hair thicker. Belle took after Papa, with blue eyes and hair so blonde that it was almost white.

"You must forgive me for coming so soon, but I was anxious to meet you and couldn't stay away. I'm Mattie Spenser, from over on the other side of Mingo." The woman had a basket on her arm, and she handed it to Carrie. "I brought you a few things to stock your cupboard—jars of preserves and jam, a smoked ham, and sourdough starter. It's so much more efficient than making yeast."

"Lizzie—" Belle started to say that Lizzie had already given them a starter. Carrie shook her head, and Belle was still.

"We're just finishing our dinner. Won't you have a cup of coffee, Mrs. Spenser?"

"Yes, if we can sit outside. The day is so glorious. I love these summer days on the plains, don't you?"

When Carrie only nodded, Mrs. Spenser said, "Well, maybe you don't yet. I imagine all this sky scares you to death. It did me when I arrived. I'd never seen anything so desolate. But that was more than forty years ago, and I have come to love it. I feel so closed in when I go back to Iowa."

"Iowa," Mama said. "We're from Iowa. Fort Madison."

"Why, so am I. You see, it may be a big world out here, but it's a small world, too. I hope we shall be great friends."

"Mrs. Spenser was a pioneer. She came here in a covered wagon nearly fifty years ago. Perhaps one day, she will tell you her stories," Papa said. "There wouldn't have been a school here without her."

"Oh, school," Belle said. She was not fond of school. She'd even thought there might not be one, that Carrie would teach them at home. Still, she loved stories. She thought maybe Mrs. Spenser would tell her stories she could write down, if only she had pencil and paper.

"Carrie's going to be a teacher," Mama said as Carrie brought out a tin cup of coffee and handed it to Mrs. Spenser.

"Carrie," Mrs. Spenser mused. "My best friend back in Iowa was named Carrie. You remind me of her."

*lll*

They all liked Mrs. Spenser. Papa said she had fought Indians and endured hardships, and that she was the first woman in Eastern Colorado to drive an automobile. She could even change a tire.

They did not care so much for Edna Hanson, however. She came that evening just before supper. Her wagon creaked and growled so much, they could hear it half a mile away.

"My goodness, we never had this much company at home. I suppose I ought to order calling cards." Mama laughed. Calling cards were pasteboard cards that fine ladies left at houses when they came to visit. Belle knew it was unlikely any of the homesteaders used calling cards.

Mrs. Hanson was a big-boned woman in a worn gingham dress that was tight around her hips and arms. Two gray braids as thin as rat tails hung below a limp sunbonnet. She had a grim look about her as she came into the soddy and glanced around, peering into the bedroom and picking up Mama's silver hand mirror. She sniffed at such an extravagant possession. Then she fingered the blue-and-white quilt Mama had put on the bed. Mama was proud of her quilts, and Belle could tell Mama expected Mrs. Hanson to compliment her on her stitching. That was what ladies did when they visited one another in Iowa. Instead the woman said, "It'll get dirty quick enough. Quilts like this are foolishness. You need practical ones, made from men's overalls, heavy as a flatiron. You'll learn."

Mama pursed her lips but didn't say anything.

"I thought I ought to call, seeing as how you're new.

Maybe give you a little advice," she said. Mrs. Hanson went over to the cupboard and studied the contents. "Looks like you got a sweet tooth for sugar," she said. It was clear she thought the Martins had no business bringing so much sweetener. She picked up the tin of cinnamon. "I could use the borrow of this. I forgot it last time I was to Mingo."

Carrie glanced at Mama, who nodded, and she sprinkled a bit of cinnamon onto a piece of paper, then folded it up and handed it to their guest.

"I guess you expect to use the rest of it," Mrs. Hanson said, as if she wanted more. Then she turned to Papa. "And Ed wants the borrow of your ax."

"I don't have it," Papa said. Belle thought she saw him wink at Mama before he added, "Ed borrowed it last week and never returned it."

Mama, who was always gracious, said, "We drank the last of the coffee, but I could make more."

"I wouldn't mind a cup, if it wouldn't rob you," Mrs. Hanson said, sitting down at the table.

Carrie said she would fix it, so she ground the coffee beans and built up the fire in the stove. Belle went outside and dipped water from the barrel. While the water boiled,

Mrs. Hanson sniffed the air. "Smells like cake," she said.

"Oh, it's all gone," Carrie said quickly. That wasn't true. Carrie had put aside a piece for the three little ones to eat after their supper, and she wasn't going to give it to the greedy neighbor.

"Slim pickin's," Mrs. Hanson muttered. She studied Carrie, then asked, "How old are you, girl?"

"Fifteen."

"I expect the boys will be sniffing around you soon. I got three of them of an age to notice girls. I reckon you'll meet them soon enough. The girls around here all take a shine to them. That Lizzie Cord is sweet on my Hugh."

Papa turned so that Mrs. Hanson couldn't see him and grinned as if to say Mrs. Hanson was crazy. "Carrie doesn't care about boys. She's going to college," he put in.

"We'll see. Plans change out here," Mrs. Hanson said. Then she got up and looked at the foodstuffs in the cupboard again and said, "I'm plum out of ginger. I don't suppose you could spare a little of that."

"We don't have any," Carrie said.

"Imagine that. No ginger."

She sat back down at the table and watched Carrie make

coffee. After a time, she looked around the room again. "I see your mister left the bare sod. Ought to put up walls. You'll get snakes coming through. And bedbugs. These walls hold bedbugs like flypaper. I bet you got them already."

Carrie handed a cup of coffee to Mrs. Hanson, who looked around until she spotted a can of evaporated milk. "Can't have coffee without milk. It sours my stomach," she said, getting up and reaching for the can. She handed it to Carrie to open. Mrs. Hanson poured a fourth of the can into her cup and drank it down. Then she stood with the can in her hand. "I'll take it with me since we're out. I was just making a neighborly call. Thought I could help you," she said, touching her sunbonnet, which covered the sides of her face. She had to turn her head to look at Mama.

"Best you get one of these," she told Carrie as she left the house. "Else your face will turn brown and wrinkled as a cow pie." She climbed into the wagon and flicked the reins on the horses' backs.

"Mrs. Hanson is sometimes given to unkind remarks," Papa said.

"I was never so embarrassed in my life," Mama said.

"Pay it no attention. Hansons are the stingiest neighbors

in the county. Borrowingest, too."

"I wonder why she came," Carrie said.

"Oh, to check you out," Papa replied.

"She didn't bring even a loaf of bread to welcome us," Mama continued.

"Well, at least she didn't bring you any more of that sourdough starter," Belle said.

Mama watched Mrs. Hanson drive away. Then, her hands on her hips, she turned to Carrie and Belle. "Girls, your father has batched here too long."

"What's batched?" Belle asked.

"It means acting like a bachelor, living by himself the way he has. Tomorrow, we will take everything out of this house and scrub the place from top to bottom."

"But, Mama, we already cleaned it. And we put things away, too," Carrie protested.

"I won't have that Mrs. Hanson saying we have bedbugs in this house! We'll clean every inch of it, then put wallpaper over the sod walls to keep out the bugs."

"Wallpaper?" Carrie asked. "We don't have wallpaper."

"You'll see," Mama said.

# Killing Bedbugs

The next morning, as soon as breakfast was over, Mama assigned chores. "Beck, there's no clothesline. I need you to set a post in the ground and string a line from it to the house."

Papa protested. He said he had work to do, but Mama told him it could wait a day. "You should have thought about a clothesline before we came. I will not spread our laundry on bushes for nosey neighbors like Mrs. Hanson to criticize. It will be hung up proper." Then she added, "But first, I want you and Frank to carry the bed and table and trunks outside. And take apart the stove, too. Everything leaves this house."

Papa and Frank went inside to dismantle the bed. Mama turned to Carrie and Belle and told them to remove the rest of the family's belongings from the house. The little ones could help, too, she added. So for an hour, everyone emptied the soddy of furniture and bedding and clothes, pots and pans and dishes and foodstuffs.

The tin dishes went into a box, where they clattered against one another. The good china dishes, Mama said, should be stacked carefully on the table. Her Haviland china was her pride. It had come from her grandmother and had been a wedding present. In seventeen years of marriage, not a single piece of it had been broken. The plates, bowls, and cups and saucers, eight of each, were white with pink rosebuds and green vines. Mama had said it was foolish to bring the china with her, but she couldn't bear to leave it behind. So she had packed the dishes in a barrel of flour to keep them from breaking. She and Carrie had already removed each piece and washed it.

Belle and Carrie removed the plates from the shelves and set them on the table that Papa had moved outside. Even little Sarah helped. She carried out the cups, holding each one in her two hands as she took tiny steps from the kitchen to the table outside, walking slowly, her eyes on the china. She set the last cup at the edge of the table, but as she turned, she bumped the cup with her elbow. It fell to the ground.

Sarah gasped, putting her little hands to her mouth in horror. The cup was broken in half, the handle smashed. "Oh, Mama," she cried, tears in her eyes.

Mama stared at the broken cup, then she slowly knelt and put the pieces into the pocket of her apron.

"I didn't mean . . . ," Sarah said.

"Of course you didn't," Mama said. She took a deep breath. "It may be the first, but it won't be the last piece of china to be broken out here. We won't cry over it, since there's not a thing we can do about it. We'll just forget it. It's my own fault for thinking I could have fine dishes out here on the prairie." She took Sarah's hands in her own and smiled at the little girl.

Belle turned to Carrie, who glanced at her then looked away, but not before Belle saw that her sister, too, was about to cry. "Mama will put those pieces into her trunk," Carrie whispered. "They're too precious to be thrown out."

*eee*

When he'd finished removing the furniture from the house, Papa dug a deep hole and set a post in it. He filled the hole with dirt and rocks, then piled rocks around the post to keep it from tipping over. Later on, after he could get to town, he would put cement in the hole to hold the post in place. He tied one end of a rope to the post and the other to the house. Carrie threw the good quilt Mama had put on the bed over the rope. Then she and Belle dumped the quilt Papa had been using since he had first arrived into a big copper boiler filled with hot water. They rubbed it against the scrub board, then rinsed it and hung it up, too. They washed Papa's dirty clothes and spread them on the sagebrush to dry. Carrie removed the old prairie grass from the bed tick Papa had used for a mattress and tossed the tick to Belle to launder. She then asked Frank to cut prairie grass to make a new mattress. Mama wiped the iron bedstead and bedsprings with coal oil, while Carrie used newspaper to scrub the soot off the kerosene lamp chimneys. Belle rubbed the stove with stove black.

When everything was clean to Mama's satisfaction, she took out a lard pail and mixed up flour-and-water paste. "Now you will see about wallpaper," she said. She brought out a stack of newspapers and magazines that Papa had saved and told Carrie and Belle to lay them on the dirt floor. The two girls spread the paste on one side of each page. Then Mama picked up the sheets one by one and pressed them against the sod walls. "Right side up, so we can read them," Mama said. The papers stuck to the layers of sod, although here and there, Mama had to put nails in the corners where they curled. "There's your wallpaper," she said when they were finished.

Papa came into the house and admired the walls. Then he read one of the newspaper headlines. "It says 'Man Found Guilty of Murdering Wife.' I guess we'll have some interesting reading of an evening."

Mama laughed. "The children will keep up with what's going on in the world. They will learn more than homesteading in this soddy."

Papa asked Frank to help him move the bed back inside, but Mama said no. They'd let the house sit for a day. Tonight they'd camp outside. They'd cook over a campfire and sleep under the moon.

"But, Louisa—" Papa protested.

Mama cut him short. "I will not have Mrs. Hanson or

anyone else say we have bedbugs, and that's that."

"But sleeping outside—"

"Not another word. You build a fire, and I'll cook dinner out here."

When the flames of Papa's fire died down, Mama and Carrie placed potatoes in the coals, along with an iron pot that contained the remains of Lizzie's beans. Then Carrie mixed up corn bread, which she poured into an iron skillet. She placed it in the coals until the corn bread was set and the edges brown. When all was ready, Mama dished up the dinner. "Be sure to eat the potato skins. They're good for you," she told the children. Mama and Papa sat on a bench Papa had brought from the barn, while the others perched on rocks to eat their supper.

When it grew dark, Mama unrolled a tarp and handed around the quilts, which had dried quickly in the hot sun. Everyone was tired, but they were too excited at the idea of spending the night under the stars to go to sleep right away. So Papa began to sing "Swing Low, Sweet Chariot," and the others joined in. Papa had a good strong voice, and Carrie's voice was rich. Belle couldn't hit any of the notes, but she made up for it by being loud. They sang "Old Folks at Home" and "Steal Away" and "Old Dan Tucker." Then one by one the little ones fell asleep.

Papa told Carrie, "Someday, I'll buy you a piano like the one you left behind in Iowa." Carrie had loved playing the piano.

She only smiled. "There isn't room for it. We'd have to put it on the soddy roof." But there was a faraway look in Carrie's eyes, and Belle knew her sister still hoped for the piano.

After a time, Papa went to the barn and came back with a long, stout rope. Placing it on the ground, he made a circle around the family.

Mama looked at him curiously. "Whatever did you do that for, Beck?"

"I tried to tell you. There are rattlesnakes out here. They say they won't crawl over a rope."

In the light from the campfire, Mama's eyes grew big. "I never thought . . . ," she said. "Maybe . . ." She raised her chin. "Well, you can't scare me, Beck. We're not going inside. I'd rather have snakes than bedbugs anytime."

It was a long while before Belle went to sleep. She looked out at the clear night, at the stars. The whole world seemed to be stars, but she wasn't thinking that just then. She looked over and saw that Carrie was awake, too. "Does a rope really stop rattlesnakes?" she whispered.

Carrie grimaced. "I don't know. I hope we don't find out."

CHAPTER FIVE

# Killing Snakes, Too

Mama worried about rattlesnakes after that, and Papa said they must keep a sharp watch for them. Bull snakes, he told them, were harmless. In fact, they ate rats and mice. But rattlers were no good.

"When God created rattlesnakes, he had a use for them, but I don't know what it was," Papa said.

Every now and then Belle and Frank spotted snake skins in the field. Papa told them that the snakes shed their skins in the spring. Belle couldn't imagine a snake wiggling out of its skin, and wondered if it looked like a great big worm until it grew a new one. But Papa explained that the new skin was in place before the snake got rid of the old one.

Frank already had spotted a rattlesnake. He and Belle were weeding the garden when he saw the snake lying in the sun. "Hey, snake!" Frank called as he threw a rock at it. The snake coiled, then raised its head, and its forked tongue went back and forth. Frank stared at the reptile's beady eyes, which seemed to hold him so that he couldn't move. Belle saw the snake too, and yelled, "Get back, Frank. He'll strike you!" As Frank jumped back, the snake struck, its long body seeming to fly through the air at the boy. Belle rushed at it with the hoe and hit the snake with the sharp edge, cutting it in half. "I don't know if it's really dead," she told her brother. "I'm going to chop it up." She hit the snake again and again until it lay in pieces.

Belle did all that without stopping to think about it. When she was finished, she began to shake. Papa, who had heard Belle warn Frank, ran up then and took the hoe from her. He put his arms around her. "You did the right thing, Bluebelle," he said. "You wouldn't think from the way it's coiled that a snake could strike such a distance. If you hadn't warned Frank, he'd have been bitten." Papa struck the end of the snake with the hoe, then reached down and picked up the rattles. "This is an old snake. You can tell by the number of rattles. I'll put them in the peach can in the barn where I keep the others. All the settlers keep the rattles."

"You've killed rattlesnakes?" Belle asked.

"Dozens of them."

"Did one ever bite you?"

"No, but there's other folks around here who have been snakebit."

Later on, Belle overheard Papa tell Mama, "Our Belle's a snake killer. She knows just what to do."

"Oh, Beck. Are there so many of them?"

"Yes, and they are everywhere, not just in the garden or the fields. I killed one in the barn, and just after I arrived here, a boy got bit by a rattler when he picked up a load of wood."

"Is he all right?"

Papa lowered his voice, but Belle could still hear him. "His mother made him drink whiskey. Then she killed a chicken and put the chicken breast over the bite. It didn't help much, however."

"Did he die?"

"He might as well have. It sapped his strength. He's not much good for anything. And his mother went loco over it. She still isn't right in her mind, and that was six months ago."

Belle heard a faint gasp and turned to see Carrie standing next to her. She had heard the snake story, too. "Doesn't that scare you?" Carrie whispered. Belle knew her sister was afraid of snakes.

The story scared Belle, but she didn't want Carrie to know that. "Don't worry. I'll kill any snake that comes around here."

ele

Belle did kill rattlesnakes, and the number of rattles in the peach can grew. But she never got over her fear of the snakes, and she watched for them wherever she was, especially around the soddy. She worried that a rattler would bite one of the younger children.

One day, Carrie was outside washing clothes in the boiler. Belle was beside her, rinsing the laundry in a second tub. She wrung out a shirt and went to the clothesline to hang it up. It was a nice day, and Mama, who was resting in bed, had asked them to take Sage's cradle outside, where the air was fresh. As Belle reached up to pin the shirt to the clothesline, she glanced down at the sleeping baby. To her horror, she saw a rattlesnake stretched out in the cradle beside Sage.

"Carrie!" she whispered because she did not know if snakes had ears. She dropped the shirt in the dirt.

Her sister looked up, puzzled. "It's all right. I can wash the shirt again," Carrie said.

"No, Carrie. The cradle. Look." Belle could barely get the words out.

Carrie glanced at the cradle then, and her eyes grew big. She let the wash fall out of her hands into the tub. "Where's Papa?" she asked.

"He's out with the horses. We have to do something. If it coils, it'll bite Sage."

Carrie stared at the snake lying beside the baby, and she began to shiver. "How do we get it out of there?"

"I don't know," Belle said. "If I try to hit the snake with the hoe, I might hit Sage instead. And the snake would get mad and bite him before I could kill it."

Carrie took a deep breath and rubbed her hands over her arms. "Maybe it'll just go away. Maybe we should leave it alone."

Belle shook her head. "I don't think so. We can't take that chance. We have to do something."

"What?"

"I don't know."

"Darn snake! I won't let it hurt Sage," Carrie said. And then before Belle could stop her, Carrie rushed to the baby's bed. She grabbed the snake by its tail, yanked it out of the cradle, and snapped it like a whip, hitting it against the ground. The snake's head broke off and flew across the dirt. Carrie flung the body as far away as she could.

Belle stared at her sister. "How did you know to do that?"

"I didn't. I just did it." She grabbed Belle and began to cry. "What if it hadn't worked? What if it'd bitten Sage?"

"But it didn't. We can't worry about what didn't happen."

"But what if . . ."

Belle shook her head. "It didn't happen, Carrie. You saved Sage from a snakebite. Maybe you saved his life."

Carrie stared at her sister for a long time. Then the two put their arms around each other until Carrie stopped crying. She dried her eyes on the sleeve of her dress. "Mama must never know," she said.

Belle nodded. She fetched her hoe and smashed the

snake's head, because she was afraid it might still contain poison. Then she found its body and dug a hole to bury the remains so that the others wouldn't see it. But before she covered the snake with dirt, she used the hoe to cut off the rattles for the peach can. They were the largest she had yet seen. Belle wished she could show them to Papa and tell him how brave Carrie had been, but she knew they wouldn't tell Papa, either.

# Lizzie's Secret

One morning, a month after the Martins were settled in, Lizzie Cord stopped at the soddy. Belle almost didn't recognize her, because Lizzie had put aside her skirt and shirtwaist in favor of men's overalls and heavy shoes. If it weren't for Lizzie's curly hair peeking out from under a man's hat, Belle would have thought she was a boy.

"Well, hello there!" she called as Belle stopped hoeing to come and greet her. "It looks like you've got a good start on the weeds. Those rows are as neat as the part in your hair."

Belle beamed—she'd worked hard to weed the garden and thin the plants and had the blisters on her hands to show it.

"Hi, Miss . . . Hi, Lizzie." Belle felt grown-up calling the visitor by her first name.

Just then Carrie came out of the soddy, and Lizzie said, "Why, Carrie, you're the one I came to see. How would you like to go into Mingo with Grover and me?" She indicated a black dog in the wagon bed. "I'm out of lard and salt pork, and lord knows what else. My coffee grinder's all busted up too, and I need a new one. It's that or smash those coffee beans with a hammer. It's a long drive, and I would be grateful for the company."

Carrie smiled. But after a few seconds, the smile faded, and Carrie shook her head. "We've too much work. There's the bread to bake, and with this stove, I can bake only two loaves at a time, so I have to make bread almost every day. And Mama's felt poorly ever since that big cleaning. She's been in bed most of the day."

Mama came to the door then. She looked thin, with dark circles under her eyes, and she hung on to the doorframe for support. Still, she said, "Go on, Carrie. I can manage fine."

"Besides, I'll be here," Belle said. It would be a grand thing to drive to town with Lizzie Cord. Belle didn't want Carrie to miss it.

But Carrie shook her head. "Becky isn't well, either. I need to stay with her. It's all Mama can do to take care of herself." She put a hand on her mother's arm. "You ought to be resting."

"I rest too much," Mama said. "You need to get out and have a little fun. You are inside this house altogether too much."

"I have fun *here*," Carrie insisted. She turned to Lizzie. "Yesterday Mama and I sat outside piecing a quilt. It's called Courthouse Steps. We love to piece. We let the time get away from us and had to scramble to fix supper. But I didn't mind. It was the nicest day I've had since we arrived."

"I'm too nervous to sit that way," Lizzie said. "I'd rather be out in the fields."

"You should see Mama's work. She could win prizes with her quilts. That horrid Mrs. Hanson—"

Mama touched Carrie's arm and shook her head.

"I mean, our good neighbor Mrs. Hanson—"

"She's horrid, all right," Lizzie broke in.

Carrie smiled. "She told Mama that making pretty quilts was a waste of time, and that Mama ought to make them out of big patches cut from blankets and men's pants."

"That's Mrs. Hanson, all right. She wouldn't appreciate your handiwork, Louisa. Beck said you were the quiltingest lady he ever saw. 'If you insult her quilts, you insult her,' he told me."

Mama smiled a little. "I guess that's about true."

"I wish you'd come along," Lizzie said as she grasped the reins and was about to slap them on the horses' backs.

"Take Belle," Carrie said suddenly. "Belle's the best company in the world, better than I am. And I bet she'd love to see the country."

Belle looked up, startled. It hadn't occurred to her that Lizzie would want to take someone as young as she was.

"Hop in, then. We want to get back before dark."

"May I, Mama?" Belle asked.

"Are your chores done?"

"All but the potato bugs." Sarah and Gully had tired of the potato bug contest, and now it was up to Belle to pick them off the plants.

"There're always potato bugs," Lizzie said. "They'll be happy to wait till tomorrow." Then she added, "Maybe there are things Belle can pick up for you at the general store."

Mama nodded. "I hadn't thought about that. I'll just

make up a list." She went inside and soon came back with a scrap of paper and a handkerchief that was knotted around some coins. She handed them to Belle, who had already climbed onto the wagon seat beside Lizzie.

"If there's anything left, get Mama a scrap of yard goods for her quilt," Carrie whispered. Most of Mama's quilts were made from leftover fabric, so store-bought material was a treat.

"I'll make sure Belle gets the best prices," Lizzie said as she slapped the reins on the horses' backs and called, "Get up, you lazy things." The horses started up at a sharp pace but slowed down by the time they got to the edge of the homestead.

"Do you like quilting, too?" Lizzie asked after they started down the road.

Belle squirmed. "My hands get sweaty, and the thread always knots up. I don't like it much."

"You're just like me," Lizzie told her.

"Don't you quilt?" Belle asked. She'd never known of a woman who didn't quilt. "What do you sleep under?"

"Oh, I have a few nice quilts that I made back in Illinois. They're in my hope chest."

"What's a hope chest?" Belle asked.

"You store quilts and embroidered linens and other pretty things in it until you're married."

"I thought you weren't going to get married."

Lizzie turned and winked at Belle. "Oh, I might someday."

"Mrs. Hanson said you'd taken a fancy to one of her sons."

"Oh, she did, did she? I'd rather marry a rattlesnake than one of them, the dirty things." She laughed and slapped the reins on the big farm horses, but they were still pokey. One of them shied, and Lizzie said, "Darn rattlesnake!" A snake slithered off to the side of the road.

Belle wanted to tell Lizzie about how brave Carrie had been when she'd whipped the snake out of Sage's cradle, but it was a secret. Instead she asked, "What about the Riley boys?" She remembered that Papa had teased Lizzie about them the day the Martin family had arrived at the soddy.

"I might as well marry a rock. Those boys don't say five words a day. That rattlesnake over there talks more than they do."

"Then who are you going to marry?"

Lizzie looked out over the land. They'd driven almost a

mile, past plowed fields as well as open prairie. She pointed
toward a shack in the middle of a field. "See that place?
There's a German man who lives there. Old Hans Kruger.
They say he's loony. I wouldn't know myself. He's always
been nice enough to me. But little children are told to stay
away from him."

"Why?"

Lizzie shrugged. "I'm not sure. It's just rumors. He came
out here with his wife and son and daughter, and the three of
them died. He was the only one who lived, and he keeps to
himself. They probably died of typhoid or pneumonia, but
some people think he killed them, others that they died of
starvation. You can do that out here when the crops fail and
there's nothing to eat but tumbleweed starts and red pepper
tea."

Belle remembered how Mama and Papa had lost their
money in Iowa. Now she wondered if the homestead failed,
whether the Martins, too, would be reduced to tumbleweeds
and hot water with red pepper.

"They say he's crazy, and whenever he sees a child, he
thinks it's one of his," Lizzie continued. "I don't know the
truth of it. There was a little boy who disappeared, and

people thought Old Hans took him."

"Did he?" Belle shivered. She didn't like the idea of such a man living near them.

"No. The boy got lost is all. He was fine when they found him. Even so, people thought Old Hans had something to do with it."

Lizzie looked at Belle as if she were afraid she'd scared the young girl. She changed the subject. "Smell the sagebrush. There's not a perfume in the world I like as much. If I ever moved away, I'd miss the smell of the sage when the rain is on it and the look of the sky at night when the stars come all the way down to the ground. This is a grand place. Whenever I hear someone say America is the land of opportunity, I believe they're talking about the Great Plains; about the idea a man—a woman, too—can come out here and get land for the price of hard work.

"Some people are frightened by the open space." She turned to Belle. "Is your sister one of them? She doesn't seem as excited about homesteading as the rest of you. I know your papa worried that the open space would frighten her."

"She's going to leave for college in a couple of years. So maybe it doesn't matter."

"I want her to like it. That's why I invited her to drive into town, so she could see the beauty of the sagebrush and the buffalo grass and the wildflowers. Even the tumbleweed. It takes time, because it's so different from what you're used to."

"I love it already," Belle said.

"That's because you're like me. I can see already that you like being outdoors." She slowed the horses and pointed to a hawk that rose out of the grass and flew off toward the sun.

"Now, that's not to say the land loves you back," Lizzie continued. "There's folks out here who've been burned out in prairie fires or had their crops dry up from lack of rain, who've near starved or who've been dusted out because of the dirt storms. I don't blame them for leaving. They don't have the strength for it. Your papa does. He'll stick. I will, too. I wasn't sure I could make it that first year when the grasshoppers ate my wheat. I got awful thin eating beans and pancakes. But I was lucky. I came out here with a little money that I'd inherited, and I didn't give up. In two more years, I'll own my homestead. Now, what do you think of that?"

Belle was silent a moment. Then she said, "I think you

didn't answer my question about who you're going to marry."

Lizzie laughed. "Aren't you the clever one! Maybe you're right. I didn't, did I?"

Belle was suddenly embarrassed that she had been so forward. Mama would tell her that Lizzie getting married wasn't any of her business. "I'm sorry. I shouldn't have asked." She hoped Lizzie wasn't sorry she'd invited Belle to drive to town with her.

"Well, don't be. I've been dying to tell someone, and I don't have any girlfriends out here. I couldn't very well confide in your papa. And Grover listens, but he doesn't talk." She glanced at the dog in the back of the wagon. "Will you keep it a secret?"

Belle nodded.

"His name is Hank Morrow. It's really Henry, but nobody calls him that. His father owns a big jewelry store in Chicago, where Hank works, and they have a mansion. He's the reason I came out here."

Belle didn't understand, but she was silent and let Lizzie continue.

"We were engaged to be married. Or the same as engaged. We grew up together and always knew we would be married,"

Lizzie said. "We weren't in any hurry, however. So I went to school for my teaching degree, and Hank worked hard in the store. His father promised to take him on as a partner. Hank's mother was dead, and Father Morrow was lonely. He didn't want Hank to get married right away, although we promised we'd live with him after the wedding. Then Hank met Iris."

Lizzie paused and again looked out over the prairie for a moment. "Her family was awfully rich. She was beautiful. I remember seeing her in the drugstore once. She was ordering French creams and lotions. They cost more than I made in a week. She kept saying she'd been to France and knew they were the very best. And maybe they were, because she had skin as white and as flawless as cream. Iris liked fine things—dresses, hats, and especially jewelry."

Lizzie shook her head a couple of times. "I introduced her to Hank. He paid her a great deal of attention, but then all the young men were smitten with her. I didn't mind. I'm not the jealous type."

A hawk swooped down, and Belle watched it catch some small animal in the field and fly off into the sky. Lizzie continued. "Then one evening, he came to my house and said he had to talk to me. He took my hand, and we went out onto the front porch and sat on the swing. I thought Hank was going to ask me to marry him. Instead he blurted out, 'I'm going to marry Iris. I asked her, and she accepted. You and I, we've always been close. At times, I thought we might marry, but of course, we were never engaged or anything. Still, I thought I ought to tell you first.' I almost burst into tears.

"'I hope you'll be happy for me,' Hank had said.

"'Yes,' I told him, although I could barely speak. 'It's just that it's so sudden.'

"Hank was almost giddy. 'When it's true love,' he said, 'I guess you know it right off.'

"I was so hurt and so angry that I stood up and told him to go home."

Belle thought that was an awful story. "I'm glad you didn't marry such a terrible person."

Lizzie smiled and smoothed Belle's hair. "At the end of the school year, I quit teaching and moved to Colorado and filed for a homestead."

"How did you know about farming?"

"I grew up on a farm, but dryland farming was new to

me. I had to unlearn much of what I knew, just like your papa. But I learned, and like I said, it won't be long before I own my homestead," Lizzie said. "I did it on my own. Without a man."

Lizzie had told Belle why she'd come to Colorado, but she hadn't said anything about who she *was* going to marry. Except it wasn't that Hank. He'd married Iris. Belle was curious, but she wasn't sure it would be polite to push Lizzie. She wished Lizzie would go on, but they were almost at town. Lizzie slapped the reins on the horses' backs and was silent.

CHAPTER SEVEN

# Belle Goes to Town

Lizzie and Belle had passed the schoolhouse a mile back. Now they entered Mingo. Belle sat back on the wagon seat and watched the town come into view. It wasn't as barren as she had first thought when she'd looked it over from the depot the day they'd arrived. She saw now that there were trees and small houses and a main street.

A stable was at the far end, and near it, a white church with a steeple. As they drove down the street, Belle saw a lumberyard and a large mercantile. There were saloons, too, and Belle heard a piano. Someone was playing ragtime music. Sometimes Carrie had played that back in Iowa, although Mama liked it better when she played hymns.

"My sister knows how to play the piano," Belle said. "Frank and I dance when she plays. But not when Mama's there."

"Your mother doesn't approve of dancing?" Lizzie asked.

"She doesn't approve of loud music."

"Well, she doesn't have to worry about that out there on the prairie."

Lizzie pulled the wagon to a stop in front of the big building and tied the horses to a railing. But instead of going into the store, she took Belle across the street to a restaurant. Belle had never eaten in a restaurant. She knew Mama hadn't given her money for a meal, and she hung back.

"My treat," Lizzie said. "I eat here once a month. It keeps me from going crazy from my own cooking." She led Belle to a table, and they sat down. Lizzie took care of the ordering, and in a minute, a woman set two plates of food in front of them—steak and mashed potatoes, both covered with heavy gravy, and green beans that were cooked to a pulp. It looked wonderful to Belle and tasted even better. Afterward, the woman brought pieces of lemon pie and coffee. Belle stared at the coffee for a moment, wondering how she could get it down. But not for the world would she let Lizzie know she didn't like it. This was turning into the best day of her life.

After dinner, the two went to the mercantile, where they each gave a list of purchases to a man behind a counter. He looked Belle over and said, "I ain't seen you before, young lady."

"She's Beck Martin's girl. They just arrived. You know her pa's got a sharp eye, so you'd best give her a good price on things."

The man grinned. "Don't I always?"

"Not so's you'd notice."

He laughed and read over Belle's list. "A bolt of muslin. I bet your ma's going to cover the ceiling of your soddy with it. Am I right?"

Belle nodded.

The man ran his finger down the list, pronouncing each item, then going to the shelves and taking it down. When he'd completed Belle's shopping, he turned to Lizzie's list. "You just got you a coffee grinder not more than a month ago, Miss Lizzie," he said.

"And it was no good. The handle broke off right away, and I can't fix it. I expect a better one this time. And I expect you not to charge me, you old skinflint."

Belle had never seen a woman barter like that, and when she paid the man from the coins in her handkerchief, she was glad Lizzie had negotiated the Martins' purchases. In fact, there was even money left over, enough for a treat, the man said.

She wandered around the store then, wondering what to buy with the last few pennies. Pa loved canned peaches, but one can wouldn't feed all the Martins. She looked longingly at a tablet. She could write down her stories in it. But the money wasn't for her. She thought about a spool of thread, but Mama had brought plenty with her. Then she saw the bolts of calico on the shelves and remembered Carrie had told her to pick a scrap of material for Mama. If the fabric had been for her, Belle would have chosen red, the brighter the better. But Mama's favorite color was yellow, the color of sunshine. So she asked the man to take down the yellow bolts, then ran her fingers over them, wondering if Mama would like the one with checks or flowers or chickens. Chickens, she decided, and asked for a quarter yard of it.

Belle handed him the coins he had given her, but he took only half of them. "Enough left for a stick of candy," he said.

She glanced around the store to see if there was anything

else to buy. And then she spotted the spools of ribbons. She loved ribbons. Red ribbons. She would buy herself a ribbon the color of sunset to tie in her pale yellow hair. She pointed to the ribbon, and the proprietor took it down. But as the man set it on the counter, Belle glanced up and saw a spool of blue ribbon. "No, that one," she said. She told the proprietor to give her as much ribbon as the remaining pennies would buy.

As they climbed into the wagon, Lizzie said, "Those are awful pretty ribbons. You'll be proud to wear them."

"Oh, they're not for me. I bought them for Carrie. They're perfect for her black hair."

Lizzie didn't say a word, but she put her arm around Belle.

ℓℓℓ

They had one more place to go, Lizzie said, stopping the wagon in front of a plain white building with a flag flying in front of it. The post office. She posted two letters, then asked for her mail and for the Martins' mail, too.

Lizzie handed Belle the letters as they got into the wagon, then picked up the reins. As they headed out of town, Belle sorted through the envelopes, looking for letters for her family, which she placed in the box with her purchases from the mercantile. She straightened Lizzie's mail and was about to put it into Lizzie's box, when she spotted a return address and the name Henry Morrow.

"Henry Morrow," she said out loud. "Is that the man . . . ?" She stopped, knowing she had overstepped. That was none of her business. *There were too many things that weren't her business*, she thought.

Lizzie only laughed. "You're too smart for your own good. I guess you'd like to know the rest of the story, wouldn't you?"

"Yes, ma'am." Belle grinned.

Lizzie took her time, looking out at the prairie. It was late afternoon by then, and the sun had turned the color of the buffalo grass to a rich yellow brown. Lizzie closed her eyes and held her face to the sun, and Belle thought about that Iris and all her creams to keep her face white. Lizzie's face was almost as tan as the grass.

"You see, Iris didn't marry Hank after all." Lizzie turned and winked at Belle. "She married his father."

"His father?"

"Yes, she'd thought Hank owned the jewelry store, but

it was Father Morrow who did, and I guess she was more interested in the jewelry than in Hank."

"So he wants to marry you again?"

"It seems so. The wedding took place not long after I left Chicago. I didn't hear about it for a long time, and by then, Hank had left Chicago, too. I didn't know where he'd gone. Not that I cared. I wasn't about to take up with him again. Besides, I was living in Colorado. Then out of the blue, about six months ago, he wrote me. He said throwing me over for Iris was the stupidest thing he'd ever done." Lizzie blushed.

"And that Hank wants to marry you?" Belle had never heard anything so romantic, better than some of the magazine stories pasted on the wall in the soddy.

"It seems so."

"Then you're leaving Colorado?" Belle didn't understand. Lizzie loved her homestead.

"I don't know, Belle. Not right now, at any rate. I want to prove up my homestead first. Still, I'd like to get married and have a family, like your family. I guess I'll have to see if he likes Colorado well enough to stay. If he doesn't, well, who knows?"

CHAPTER EIGHT

# A Homesteader Party

In August, Mrs. Spenser sent out invitations to a birthday party. She wanted everybody to come and meet her grand-daughter, Hazel, who was visiting from Denver. Hazel, who was turning four, was spending a month with her.

The Spensers had come to Colorado in 1865 to start a farm, but they had become ranchers. Over the years, they had bought the land of busted-out homesteaders and now had the biggest cattle spread in Bondurant County. Lizzie told the Martins that the Spensers would slaughter a calf for the party, then barbecue it in a pit. They would serve it with potatoes and potato salad, corn and beans and baked beans, tomatoes and cucumbers and lettuce. Dessert would be cake and ice cream made with peaches shipped from over the mountains to the far west. It would be the highlight of the summer. The men would talk about crops and cattle, and the women about quilts and canning and who was getting married or having a baby. The children would play in the big grassy yard. Many hadn't seen grass since they'd moved to Colorado. Then there would be dancing and singing.

"They have the best parties in Bondurant County," Lizzie said, then thought a minute. "They have the only real parties, too."

"Putting on airs with those written invitations. What's wrong with just telling everybody to come?" Mrs. Hanson complained. She had been driving down the road in her squeaky wagon. When she saw Lizzie and Mama outside the soddy, she turned in and drove the few hundred feet to the soddy. She climbed out of the wagon, ready to gossip. "Why, how much do you think they spent on stamps? I say that's the waste of a good dollar. Maybe more."

"Written invitations are a courtesy. They're good manners," Mama replied. Mrs. Spenser had been kind to the Martins, and Mama was quick to defend her. "She is honoring us. She is a fine lady."

"It's show-offy, if you ask me," Mrs. Hanson said. She didn't seem to like what Mama had said, so she got back into her wagon. "Showing off how much money she has."

"Is Mrs. Spenser rich?" Belle asked after Mrs. Hanson was out of hearing.

"She certainly has more money than the rest of us do," Lizzie said. "Yes, I suppose the Spensers are rich, but nobody begrudges it. They settled this country, and they helped folks who came after them. They loaned money to some of the homesteaders when they were busted out and didn't even charge interest. They don't act high-and-mighty about it, either. Mr. Spenser visits around and gives advice on crops and livestock."

In fact, Luke Spenser had stopped at the Martins' homestead to ask how things were going and to suggest Papa rotate his crops every two or three years. And he'd asked Papa's advice about a horse he was thinking of buying. That made Papa feel pretty good.

"The Spensers always seem to know when you need something," Lizzie continued. "One day when I was down in the dumps and so lonely that I was ready to give up, Mrs. Spenser came to visit me and brought me Grover. He was a puppy then. She said she had a feeling I might like to have him for company. Grover was the pick of the litter. Why, he made me feel better right away. What got me was how she knew that particular day was just about the lowest of my life. I expect she went through some hard times, too." Lizzie reached down and patted Grover's head. "So I say, if they're rich, hooray for them."

ℓℓ℮

The Martins talked about the upcoming party for two weeks. Mama and Carrie got out their best dresses and steamed the flounces and ribbons over the teakettle. They heated the heavy black irons on the stove and pressed everyone's clothes. Belle had only three dresses. Still, she went back and forth, trying to choose which one was the nicest. She decided on a red-checked gingham that had belonged to Carrie and been cut down to fit her. Mama took a swath of red fabric from the trunk and made a sash for it. "You ladies will be all bugged up," Papa said.

The day of the party, Mama and Carrie rose before dawn and bathed in the washtubs. Then they gave the younger children baths and dressed them in their good clothes. They were all nervous about the party.

Just as Belle and Carrie had finished dressing, Belle opened the trunk where she stored her treasures and took out the blue hair ribbons. She had been saving them for a special occasion. "For you," she said, handing them to Carrie.

"They will look so pretty in your hair," Carrie told her.

"No, they're for you. I bought them in town."

"For me?" Carrie took the bright ribbons and slowly ironed them between her fingers. When she looked up at Belle, her eyes glowed. "How did you know I always wanted blue hair ribbons?" There was a catch in her voice.

Belle shrugged. "I didn't. I just thought . . ."

"You're the best sister in the world," Carrie told her. She went to the mirror, then slowly tied the ribbons around her braids.

As Belle was tying her sash, Frank said, "You look prissy."

"Do not!" Belle threw a dirt clod at him.

"Do too." Frank threw one back, and before anyone could stop them, they were in a dirt clod fight.

"I ought to leave you home as punishment," Mama said.

"I'm sorry," Belle said, hanging her head. "I guess I'm

just excited."

"Louisa, I think it would be rude if we didn't all show up, since you accepted the invitation for all of us," Papa said. "Besides, the children are likely to get dirty there anyway."

Mama sighed. "I guess you're right."

Papa turned away and winked at Belle and Frank.

Carrie dusted off Belle's dress and told her the dirt was barely visible. They all climbed into the wagon and drove to Lizzie's soddy, because she was going to ride to the party with them. She was waiting at the road, dressed in her black skirt and shirtwaist and wearing a straw hat that was as big as a washtub. It had a white feather sticking straight up and might have been the most stylish hat Belle had ever seen. Lizzie lived in a soddy, but she knew how to get bugged up, as Papa had put it. Lizzie subscribed to *Ladies' Home Journal* and gave the copies to Carrie when she was finished. Now she looked just like she'd come out of one of the magazine pages. Belle wondered if Lizzie kept up on fashions in case Hank came to visit her.

Everybody had been invited to the Spensers' party, so there were other wagons on the road. They passed a Reo automobile that had slid into the ditch and was being pulled out by a team of horses. A man stood beside the car, looking embarrassed. Frank called out, "Get a horse!" as they passed. Everybody laughed. That was what people always yelled to a man whose motorcar had broken down.

There were other wagons and a few motorcars and trucks at the Spensers' ranch when the Martins arrived. Papa helped Mama down from the wagon, and Carrie handed her a raisin pie they had baked that morning. Papa had said they didn't need to bring food, that the Spensers would have enough for the whole county. Mama said she wouldn't think of going to a party empty-handed. Other women felt the same way, as Belle saw them carrying pies and cakes and cobblers to a big table. Belle made it a point to remember Mama's pie so that she could have a piece. That was because Mama was a good cook. It was also because Mama would feel insulted if any of her pie was left when the party was over.

Mrs. Spenser, wearing a big apron wrapped around her, came to greet them. She held the hand of a little girl and introduced her as her granddaughter.

Hazel didn't look up when her grandmother said her name. "She's shy," Mrs. Spenser told them. "I wish she would play with the other children, but she clings to me."

Mama and Papa left with Becky and baby Sage to put the pie on the table. Carrie knelt down next to Hazel. "Hazel is such a pretty name. Do you know how to spell it?"

The girl stared at Carrie's blue hair ribbons instead of looking at her. She was still for a long time. Finally she said, "No."

"That's all right," Carrie said. "Sarah doesn't know how to spell her name, either, and I'm going to teach her this very minute." She took Hazel's hand, then motioned for Sarah to follow her. Gully tagged along too, although he could spell his name. Carrie sat down on a large rock and picked up a stick. She wrote "Sarah" and "Hazel" in the dirt. "That's Sarah's name, and that's your name, Hazel. Can you see anything in the two names that is the same?"

After a time, Sarah pointed to the letter "A."

"That's right," Carrie said.

"She has two of them. I have only one," Hazel said. "How come?"

"Because your names are different."

"I want to tell Grandfather," Hazel said, and jumped up. "Come on," she told Sarah and Gully. "You can tell him your letters, too."

Mrs. Spenser watched the three race off. "A minute ago, she was so shy, she wouldn't let go of me. Now she's a completely different child. You are a wonder with children, Carrie. You will make a fine teacher."

## CHAPTER NINE

# Mrs. Spenser's Gift

❧

School started late in the fall, because most of the homestead boys and girls had to stay home to help with the harvest. The older Martin children worked in the fields with their father to harvest their crops, although the result was poor. Papa was still learning about dryland farming.

"I thought we would do better. I haven't gotten the hang of dryland farming yet," Belle heard Papa tell Mama. "It means a lean year ahead of us."

"We will manage," Mama said. "We always have."

Papa patted her hand. "Thanks to you."

The five older children were enrolled in the school, which was nearly two miles away. Sometimes Papa drove them in the wagon, but most of the time they walked. The horses were needed on the farm. The long walk was hard on the two youngest children, Sarah and Gully, and often the others stopped so that they could rest.

"I don't know what we'll do when winter comes," Carrie confided to Belle. "The little ones won't be able to tramp through the snow all the way to school."

"They'll have to stay home," Belle replied.

"We'll all have to stay home. Mama's doing so poorly that she can barely take care of Becky and the baby by herself."

"Then Papa will just have to let us take the wagon."

Carrie sighed. She had been working sums on a piece of wrapping paper. "He won't. He doesn't have time to drive us every day, and he needs the horses at home."

"Mama will make him take us," Belle said.

"No." Carrie shook her head. "I'm not sure he believes that going to school is that important."

Belle raised her head and stared at her sister. "He doesn't?"

"It's Mama who wants us to go to school. She says you can't get anywhere without an education." Carrie looked around, then whispered, "If Papa had gone to high school, he might have gotten a job back in Iowa, maybe at a bank or a farm store, and we wouldn't have had to move here. But he didn't have that chance, because farming is all he knows."

Belle had never thought about that. She loved her father. Carrie did, too. He was the best man they knew—the kindest, the smartest, the hardest working, and the gentlest. Why, he never even whipped them when they were bad. "Maybe he didn't want to go to school. Maybe he always wanted to farm. Is that why you want to go to college, so you won't have to be a farmer's wife?"

"Oh, Belle, I want to go because I love to learn, and if I learn, I can teach. Mama wants me to go to college, too. She wants all of us to go. She expects me to graduate, then help you, and then we'll both help Frank."

Belle nodded. Except for reading and writing stories, she didn't like school much, but she liked learning things, too. Even when she'd thought about Carrie teaching them at home, Belle had assumed that would be temporary. She couldn't imagine that they wouldn't be able to go to school at all.

ℓℓℓ

Belle remembered that conversation during snowy days. At first, it was fun walking to school, bundled up against the cold, stopping to throw snowballs at Frank or making snow angels. But after a time, they all grew to dislike the long walk down the icy dirt road. The snow swirled around them and sent pinpricks of ice against their skin. Sometimes when the snowfall was heavy, they stayed home. Papa said it was too dangerous for them to walk to school, that they could be caught in a ground blizzard and wander off the road and get lost. Belle knew that meant they could freeze to death, and the thought frightened her.

"Will we have to stay home all winter?" she asked Carrie.

"I don't know."

The children had already missed several days due to the weather. On a day in mid-December when the snow was too thick for them to leave the soddy again, Carrie put her head in her hands. She had been sitting at the table, helping Belle with her sums. She didn't often get discouraged, so Belle knew something was wrong. "What is it?" she whispered.

"I'm just tired."

"No, what is it?"

Carrie looked around the room to make sure Mama wasn't listening. "If I can't go to school, I won't graduate, and then how can I go to college? Oh, Belle, it's so disappointing."

Belle tried to think of something to say but couldn't. She took her sister's hand to show she cared. They sat there for a long time.

Then they heard an automobile outside. Belle drew aside the curtain over the window and peered out. They hadn't known that the snow had stopped and the sun was shining. The window was small, and it was dark in the soddy.

Mama heard the car, too, and went to the door and opened it. "Why, it's the Spensers. Quick, Carrie, get out the bread and butter for our guests. And make coffee, too." Mama stepped outside and called, "You've brightened our day as much as the sun." Then she turned to Frank. "Go get your father from the barn."

"No, I'll go there," Mr. Spenser said. "I need to ask his advice. I've got a mule that's ailing, and the animal doctor's gone to Denver. Maybe your husband will know what to do about it. You go inside and get warm, Mattie," he told his wife, squeezing her arm with affection.

"I *will* go inside. My hands are frozen to my gloves," Mrs. Spenser said. She went into the soddy and took off her coat. "I should have made Luke drive the buggy and let me take the car."

"You brought both your buggy and your motorcar?" Belle asked. She exchanged a look with Carrie. Why would they do such a thing?

"Yes, and now I know why we bought an automobile. I'm too old to go off in this cold with a buggy. Come and sit in my lap, Sarah, and tell me how to spell your name. Maybe one day, you and Hazel will write letters to each other."

Sarah climbed into Mrs. Spenser's lap and slowly said, "S-A-R-A-H."

"She's quite the scholar," Mrs. Spenser said when Carrie handed her a tin cup of coffee.

Belle couldn't stand it any longer. "Why did you come here in both an automobile and a buggy?" she asked.

Mrs. Spenser looked up from Sarah. "Oh, I guess I didn't tell you. That old buggy has been sitting in our barn so long, it's wearing out from lack of use. I thought you could drive it back and forth to school. It would be a kindness if you'd take it off my hands. One more thing I wouldn't have to worry about."

"You're giving us the buggy?" Belle asked.

"If you'll take it."

"It's much too valuable. We can't accept," Mama said.

"Why, of course you can. The buggy's no use to me sitting in the barn. And your children need a way to get to school. You and I both know how important an education is. Even in this day and age when women in Colorado have the vote, they still don't have many options for employment. With a college education, Carrie could do all kinds of things. You wouldn't deprive her of that, would you?"

Before Mama could reply, Carrie put her hands to her mouth. "That's wonderful, Mrs. Spenser! How can we thank you?"

"By going to school."

"But how can we do that? We can't pull the buggy ourselves," Belle put in. "Papa won't let us have one of his horses. He needs them on the farm."

"Of course he does. Besides, a big old farm horse is too plodding to pull a buggy. That's why I brought the pony." She turned to Frank. "He'll have to be your responsibility, young man. You'll take care of him, won't you? Rub him down every night and put a blanket over him when he stands in the cold in the school yard. I believe he needs a boy to ride him sometimes, too." She looked at Belle. "And maybe a girl, too. His name is Catsup, because he's red."

Frank stood with his mouth open, too excited to speak.

"I don't know what to say," Mama told her.

"You don't have to say anything, Mrs. Martin. I just want to make sure these boys and girls go to school. Someday Carrie is going to make us all proud of her, and I would like to claim a little of the credit."

# A Colorado Christmas

e⌢9

One morning in late December, after Papa and Frank had fed the animals and milked June, the Martins were sitting around the table eating breakfast. Mama asked, "Has everybody forgotten Christmas is coming?"

Belle hadn't forgotten. But she knew that money was scarce, that everything they had went toward food. So there was nothing left to spend on presents. Besides, they had left their ornaments and decorations back in Iowa. "I thought we were going to forget Christmas this year," she said.

"Forget Christmas?" Mama replied. "Why, I never heard of such a thing."

"But the money—" Belle said. She knew things were so

tight that they no longer purchased sugar and cinnamon and ginger.

"Money! What does money have to do with Christmas? It's a time to celebrate and to give thanks for all of our blessings." Mama turned to Papa. "We have so many, don't we, Beck? I can count seven of them right here in this room." She glanced around at the children, stopping to smile at Sage sleeping in his cradle. She pulled Becky onto her lap.

"Will we have a Christmas tree?" Frank asked.

"There aren't any trees out here, and if there were, Papa wouldn't cut them down," Belle told him.

"We'll have a Christmas bush," Carrie said. "Mrs. Spenser said that's what she had her first Christmas in Colorado. I will put together the bush if Belle will help, and the other children can make the ornaments."

The day before Christmas, the two girls went outside and searched for the best and biggest tumbleweeds they could find. It wasn't hard, as they were scattered all across the farm. They fitted the bushes together until they were the shape of an evergreen tree as tall as the ceiling of the soddy. Then Carrie mixed up a batch of starch, and they carefully painted the tumbleweed tree with the starch until it was as white as a snowflake.

Meanwhile, Frank took out the scissors and a copy of Lizzie's *Ladies' Home Journal,* and the little ones cut out pictures of animals and children, of birds and stars and even candy. They carefully poked the sharp edges of the tumbleweeds through the pictures. That night Papa took out a sack of kernels he had purchased at the mercantile and built up a hot fire in the stove. He dumped the contents of the sack into a cast-iron frying pan.

"Popcorn!" Belle said. "We'll make popcorn strands."

They stood around the stove, jumping a little as the first kernels began to pop. When the popping stopped, Mama brought out her needle and thread, and the children took turns threading the popped corn until it made up a long string. Then Carrie wrapped it around the tree. They all gathered about to admire it.

"Best Christmas tree we ever had," Belle said.

"We just need presents," Frank told her.

Mama and Papa looked at each other.

"We don't need presents. We have each other," Carrie spoke up.

*They were lucky for that,* Belle told herself as she went

to sleep that night. She wished the little ones could have Christmas presents, but they didn't even have the colorful Christmas stockings they had once hung up on Christmas Eve. Perhaps that didn't matter, because it was unlikely Saint Nicholas would know they'd moved to Colorado. But then, Belle didn't believe in Saint Nick.

ℓℓℓ

"Belle!" Frank whispered. "Wake up."

The soddy was cold. It was always cold on winter mornings before Papa or Carrie made a fire in the stove. Belle snuggled under the quilt and put her cold feet against Carrie. They all wore stockings to bed now. And sweaters. "Go away, there's no school today," Belle muttered.

"Saint Nicholas came," he whispered.

*Frank doesn't believe in Saint Nick, either,* Belle thought. But she roused herself and searched for her shoes on the dirt floor beside the bed. Frank stood there, holding a pocket-knife in his hand. It was red and had two blades, one large, the other small. Belle had seen him staring at one exactly like it at the mercantile.

"Somebody hung up my stocking, and I found this in it. Your stocking's up there, too."

Belle stared at the soddy wall where seven stockings hung. One *was* hers, and she glanced down at her feet to discover that her left foot was bare. Frank, too, was wearing only one stocking. "Somebody took them off when we were sleeping," she whispered. She nudged her sister. "Get up, Carrie. Look," she said when Carrie opened her eyes. Belle pointed to the wall. "Did you do that?"

"Do what?" Carrie looked bewildered.

"The stockings."

Carrie pushed aside the quilts and stood up. She, too, had on a single stocking.

By then, the little ones were awake, and Frank pointed to the stockings. "Saint Nicholas came last night."

The children rushed to take down their stockings and pull out the contents—rag dolls for Sarah and Becky, a rubber ball for Gully. For Sage there was a stick with a small tin can attached. The can was filled with pebbles. "A rattle," Belle said. Inside Carrie's stocking was a small book. It was worn and the cover water-stained, but it was a book! Carrie held it against her heart.

Belle's stocking was limp, and she wondered if she had been overlooked. Then she glanced at the floor beneath her stocking. There was the tablet of paper she had wanted to buy at the mercantile in the summer. She glanced over at Mama, who watched her with shining eyes.

"A notebook," Belle said, picking it up.

"So you can write down our stories, Bluebelle," Mama said.

ee

That afternoon, Lizzie came to the soddy. She was going to ride to the school with the Martins. Papa had turned the sledge he used to haul sod into a sleigh. The children were putting on a special Christmas program. Lizzie was bugged up in her shirtwaist and black skirt. She wore a ring with a big blue stone in it and a brooch with tiny pearls and sparkly stones.

"Diamonds," Carrie whispered to Belle.

"Is that like glass?" Belle asked.

"No. Even better. They're precious stones, and they cost a great deal of money."

Belle wondered if Lizzie's friend, Hank, had given her the jewelry. After all, Lizzie had said his father owned a jewelry store. But of course, she couldn't ask just then. Carrie didn't know about Hank, and Lizzie had never mentioned him again.

The school was decorated with wreaths made of twigs, since there were no evergreens around Mingo. Cutout letters spelling "Merry Christmas" hung above the blackboard. There was the smell of apple cider. The Spensers had set a huge kettle of it on the stove to warm. There were cookies and cakes, too. Mama brought a cake made with the last of the cinnamon.

The children sang Christmas songs and then performed in a play based on the Christmas story. The tallest boy in the school played Joseph, while Carrie was Mary. The two went around the room, asking for a place to spend the night. Children, acting the parts of villagers, turned them away. Finally Frank said they could stay in his stable, and Mary and Joseph went behind a quilt hung across the room.

A minute later, Belle and another girl drew the quilt aside, and there sat Mary and Joseph with the baby Jesus in a cradle. The baby was really Sage.

Everyone clapped, and Mrs. Spenser told Mama that Sage made a perfect Holy Child.

"Until he began to cry," Mama said.

Mrs. Spenser started to reply, but just then they heard sleigh bells. There was a loud knock on the door. A man entered dressed as Saint Nicholas, with a beard that looked like it was made of cotton and an elaborate coat. He looked a great deal like Mr. Spenser.

He carried a big sack, and he gave each child a candy stick and a dime. Sarah and Gully had never had dimes before, and they ran to Mama and showed them to her. "I never heard of anything so generous," Mama told Mrs. Spenser. And then she whispered, "Thank you."

Afterward, everyone gathered around the stove for refreshments. Lizzie cut the cakes and handed around slices, her pretty ring twinkling on her hand. The schoolhouse was jammed with people, not just the families of students but everyone in the county, it seemed. Belle saw several rough-looking men dressed in filthy clothes and wondered who they were. One of them was watching Lizzie. Mama told her not to stare at them. It was Christmas and everyone was welcome. After all, she added, Christmas was about love and peace.

That night, as the Martins and Lizzie drove home in the sleigh, they sang Christmas carols. The dark night was lit only by the stars.

"Best Christmas we ever had," Mama said as they stopped to let Lizzie out at her soddy.

"I wouldn't trade Christmas with you for anything in the world," Lizzie replied. Belle felt the same way.

# Staying with Lizzie

Early in the new year, the weather turned bitterly cold, so cold that for a week, the Martin children stayed home from school. Papa said the pony Catsup shouldn't stand outside in the freezing weather all day, and Mama was afraid they would get sick traveling the nearly two miles to school in such bad weather. The water in the barrel outside the door froze, and each morning Papa had to break loose chunks of ice with an ax. He put them into a kettle set on the hot stove to melt. In the summer, he said, he would see about drilling a well. It was even cold in the soddy, so cold that Carrie and Belle slept with the bowl of sourdough starter between them to keep it from freezing.

At first, the children played games inside. Carrie read to them, and Belle used her hands to make shadow pictures on the wall. But they got bored with being cooped up and began to squabble, so Mama bundled them up and sent them out into the cold to play or work in the barn. Belle and Frank curried Catsup and the two workhorses, and they helped Papa feed the animals.

Lizzie came over one day and said it was so cold that she'd brought the chickens inside her soddy. She was afraid they would freeze, although she admitted she liked their company. "I was going stir-crazy, just me and Grover," she said. "I got so I was talking to the chickens. I think they liked that because they clucked to agree with everything I said. Oh, to have a talking machine." She had seen a picture of a Victrola in the Sears, Roebuck catalog.

Becky, who had wandered outside without her coat on and fallen in the snow, had developed a fever. Mama, who was sick herself, treated her with honey and coal oil. "But it doesn't seem to make a difference," Mama said.

Lizzie told her she had some snakeroot and tramped back through the snow to her soddy to fetch it.

"You are a godsend," Mama said after Lizzie returned.

"You must take some yourself," Lizzie insisted. "You're no good to anybody if you're sick, too. As soon as the road is clear, I'll go into town and ask the doctor."

"Beck already went," Mama said. "The doctor isn't much good. He said the cold had to run its course."

"You fear pneumonia," Lizzie told her.

Mama nodded.

Lizzie came every day after that. *She is indeed a godsend,* Belle thought. With money so scarce, the Martins were living on beans and bread. Lizzie brought soup that she'd made with potatoes and turnips that were stored in the cellar she'd had dug behind her house. The next week Lizzie went into town and bought a piece of meat, which she boiled to make beef broth for Becky. Once she gave Becky an orange. The Martins hadn't seen oranges since they moved to Colorado, and the other children gathered around to see Becky eat it. Carrie saved the peel, which she carved into slivers and baked with flour and water and sourdough starter into a kind of bread-cake.

ᘢ

Becky didn't improve. Mama slept only a little, because she was so worried. And she feared that Sage would catch his sister's cold. Sage had begun to crawl, and he liked to climb into bed with Becky to keep warm. Mama would put him back into his cradle, but he always got out and sneaked into bed with his sister.

"He's so little, I'm afraid what would happen if he got sick," Mama told Lizzie. Mama was coughing, too, and she turned her face away from Sage. "He could catch it from me, as well."

Lizzie thought a moment. "I could take him to my place and keep him there. Trouble is, I don't know anything about taking care of babies. I was the youngest in my family."

"I could watch him," Belle spoke up. "I could go to Lizzie's house and tend him."

Lizzie clapped her hands. "What a grand idea. I should love the company. It gets lonely on these cold nights with only Grover and the chickens for company."

Belle was so excited that right away she began gathering the baby's cup and clothes and cans of evaporated milk. She placed them in the cradle. Mama wrapped Sage in a quilt and handed him to Lizzie. Then Papa loaded the cradle into the wagon, hitched the horses, and drove them to Lizzie's house.

"I'll send Frank every day to tell you how Becky is doing," he told them as he left.

Lizzie's large one-room soddy was quiet and neat. At least it was after they got rid of the chickens. Belle thought it was enchanting. There were no children underfoot, no yelling and talking, no toys cluttering the floor. Lizzie had pretty flowered curtains at her window, which was made of four panes of glass. A crocheted rug covered the floor in front of the bed so that Lizzie didn't have to step out on a dirt floor in the morning. A rope was stretched across a corner of the room where clothes hung on wire triangles. They were called hangers, Lizzie explained. Belle had never seen them before.

A fancy iron bed was covered with half a dozen quilts. The top one was made of a single piece of white cloth, stitched in an intricate design. Belle smiled when she remembered Mrs. Hanson criticizing Mama for having a blue-and-white quilt, which she'd said would only get dirty. Belle fingered the spread.

"Do you like quilting any better now?" Lizzie asked.

Belle shook her head. "I'd rather work in the garden or ride a horse."

"Me too, but quilting is something to do on winter

nights when I can't sit outside."

Belle had taken the baby things out of the cradle, and now she laid Sage in it for his nap.

"Let me show you what I'm working on now. It's called a Crazy Quilt. It's useless out here on the prairie, but not everything has to be practical." Lizzie opened a trunk and took out a patchwork of silks and velvets cut into odd shapes, stitched together like a giant puzzle. The seams were covered with gold embroidery in a variety of stitches. The colors shone like jewels in the light of the kerosene lamp, and Belle couldn't help but run her hand over the fabric. "What's that ribbon?" she asked. She pointed to a strip of silk covered with writing.

"I won that in school. I placed second in a footrace. Girls weren't supposed to run, but the judges couldn't find anything written down that disqualified me. So they had to give me a ribbon. Hank—I told you about him—thought it was scandalous."

"Good for him. You won fair and square."

"No, he thought it was scandalous that I entered the race. He expected me to give back the ribbon."

"I'm glad you didn't."

"He's coming to see me. In the spring." Lizzie turned away to hide her blushing face.

"Are you going to marry him?"

Lizzie didn't answer. She ran her hand over the bright squares of the quilt, then set it on top of the trunk. "He hasn't asked me."

"I bet he will," Belle said. "Anybody would be glad to marry you. I'm sure that's why he's coming to see you."

Lizzie smiled. "I think so, too."

"Will you say yes?"

"I don't know. I get lonely out here, even with Grover." She reached down and patted the dog. "When I go to your house and see how happy you are, I know I want what you have. Still, I don't want to leave Colorado. I don't know if I can go back to wearing corsets and drinking tea in closed-up parlors. And sewing's nice for an evening, but I want to work in the fields."

"Maybe Mr. Morrow will buy a farm in Illinois."

"I've thought about that. I think that's what's called a compromise." Lizzie laughed. "Now I'm compromising on something else. I'm completely out of sugar, so we'll have to use corn syrup to sweeten a cake we're going to make.

Is that all right with you?"

Belle grinned. "That's swell. We haven't had sugar since way last fall. Mama says it's too expensive."

"Are things that hard?" Lizzie asked.

Belle nodded. "I think you know the harvest wasn't as good as Papa had hoped." Then she said quickly, "We don't mind. Everything will be better after the harvest next year."

Lizzie took Belle's hands and asked, "Are you living on corn bread and beans?"

"Wheat bread, too." Belle looked away. She didn't want her friend to know how desperate the Martins were. Just a few nights before, when her parents had thought she and Carrie were asleep, she had heard Papa say that if the harvest wasn't any better next year, they might have to use Carrie's college fund to buy seed.

"Over my dead body! That was my inheritance, and it's to go to Carrie for her schooling, even if I starve!" Mama had said.

"But you need things, too," Papa had told her. "I saw you mending your skirt. You're putting patches on patches."

"It doesn't matter. Carrie is going to college," Mama had replied.

Carrie had been awake, too, and when Belle touched her sister's face, she felt tears. But of course, Belle didn't tell that to Lizzie. She didn't want her to pity the Martins.

Supper with Lizzie that night was such a treat that Belle felt almost guilty. It had been a long time since the Martins had eaten meat. Lizzie said the steak was tough and tasteless—although she had paid twenty-four cents a pound for it!—but Belle thought it was delicious. The cake was a great success, too. Lizzie declared they would make another for the Martins the next day. Frank could take it home when he visited with news of Becky. After supper, as they listened to coyotes wail far away, Lizzie stitched on the Crazy Quilt while Belle read out loud from *The Little White Bird*. She was intrigued with the story of a little boy called Peter Pan, who didn't want to grow up. And she liked reading it to Lizzie. Someday, perhaps, she would write her own stories. Maybe she'd write one about Lizzie.

That night, Belle slept with Lizzie in a real bed, not a pallet on the dirt floor, and between sheets, too. The Martins hadn't had sheets since Iowa.

ele

Frank rode Catsup to Lizzie's soddy every day with news of Becky. He brought schoolwork, too. The weather had improved and the other children had returned to school. But Belle was staying away to care for Sage. Frank left with soup or a cake that Lizzie and Belle had made. Becky was worse, and Belle wanted to go home to see her. But Mama sent word for Belle to stay away for fear she would catch Becky's sickness and give it to Sage. Frank had been told to keep his distance from the baby, too.

Despite her worry for her little sister, Belle was happy staying with Lizzie. She fed the chickens, which didn't seem to mind being back in their coop, and helped care for Lizzie's horses. She swept the soddy. Then she and Lizzie took down the muslin tacked to the ceiling, threw out the dirt that had fallen on it, washed it, and tacked it back in place.

Best of all were the evenings, when the two sat at the table and sewed and read until they were too sleepy to keep their eyes open. "You are just like a sister to me," Lizzie said, which Belle thought might be the nicest thing anyone had ever told her. She had grown to love Lizzie almost as much as she did Carrie.

# The Intruder

Belle had stayed with Lizzie for almost a week when she woke up in the middle of the night to the sound of a horse neighing just outside the soddy. She knew Lizzie's animals were secure in the barn, so the visitor must be Frank. Or Papa. They would be bringing bad news. Good news would have waited until morning.

She climbed out of bed, hoping she wouldn't wake Lizzie, but Lizzie put her hand on Belle's arm and whispered, "Wait."

The dog began to growl.

"It's all right, Grover. I think it's Frank," Belle said.

"I'm not so sure," Lizzie told her.

The two sat on the edge of the bed. Belle listened as hard as she could for someone to knock, while Grover whined to go outside. After a moment, she decided Lizzie was right. The horse's neigh didn't sound like Catsup's. Besides, if Papa or Frank had come, they would have called out. Instead, except for the horse, everything was silent.

"It might be somebody needing help. Maybe one of the Rileys or the Hansons," Belle whispered.

"If it was, he'd call, 'Hello, the house.' "

In a minute, they heard someone at the door. Whoever it was didn't knock. Instead it seemed that he was trying to be as quiet as snow as he opened the door. But the door held. There were brackets on the inside wall on either side of the door, and Lizzie had put a board through them, barring the door. Still, Belle was aware that with enough force, the brackets could pull out of the sod wall. She hoped the man didn't know that.

"It's someone up to no good," Lizzie said. She stood and quickly went to a trunk and opened it. She lit a candle. Then she took out a shotgun and began loading it. Her hands were shaking. When she was finished, she called, "Git, you! My husband and I have guns."

"Then open the door. I got a sick woman out here."

*Maybe we are wrong,* Belle wondered. *What if someone really is sick?*

But Lizzie whispered, "Don't fall for that. I'm sure he's alone. Can you peek out the window?"

Belle went to the window and drew aside the curtain and peered out. The man was indeed alone. In the moonlight, he looked familiar, but she wasn't sure where she had seen him. And then she remembered. "He was one of the strangers at the school at Christmas."

"He's after my jewelry. When he admired my ring, I thought I was foolish to wear it. He gave me a bad feeling," Lizzie said.

"You ain't got a husband in there. You're a spinster lady," the man called. He turned and looked directly at Belle before she could drop the curtain. "Looks like you got a little girl with you. You don't want her to get hurt, so you open that door. If I have to break it down, you won't like it." The man reached into his saddlebags, and when he turned toward the house, he had a gun in one hand and a hammer in the other. "Girlie, you open that door. Ain't nobody here to protect you."

"What do we do?" Belle looked at Lizzie, then glanced at

Sage. She was grateful he was asleep in his cradle.

"I don't know," Lizzie whispered. "He means to harm us."

"This is your last chance," the man called.

Belle glanced again at Lizzie. "Will you really shoot him? Papa says a gun is for shooting coyotes and rattlesnakes, not people."

"That man's no better than a rattlesnake. Besides, he could hurt you. Or Sage. I can't let him do that. Blow out the candle." When the soddy was dark, Lizzie told Belle to pull back the curtain.

Belle hesitated. "Maybe he'll ride away."

"He won't."

Belle pushed aside the curtain.

"Get out of the way," Lizzie ordered Belle. She aimed the shotgun at the window and pulled the trigger.

Glass from the window shattered and there was a scream. The two knew Lizzie had hit the man. Lizzie began shaking. "I only wanted to scare him and make him ride off," she said.

Belle was too frightened to look outside. Although the man was bad, she hoped he was all right. "Don't die. Please don't die," she muttered.

"He won't die," Lizzie said, pushing Belle aside so that she could peer out the window. "Look, he's getting on his horse."

The man put his foot into the stirrup and swung his other leg over his horse. Then he picked up the reins, using only one arm. The other hung down at his side.

"I think I shot him in the arm," Lizzie said as the man rode off.

Belle wanted to go outside, to make sure the man was gone, but Lizzie told her to wait until dawn.

Neither of them went back to sleep. After a time, Lizzie built up the fire in the stove and made coffee. This time, Belle liked its strong flavor. When daylight finally came, they opened the door and looked around. There were horse tracks in front of the soddy, and they found drops of blood in the snow. But there was no sign of the man.

"We have to tell your parents. You were very brave. He might have murdered us—and Sage," Lizzie said, glancing at the baby, who had slept through the entire ordeal.

"No, we can't tell them. Mama would be frightened. Carrie, too. And after I go home, they would worry about you being here alone."

Lizzie thought that over. "We'll have to inform the sheriff. We don't want that man hurting anyone else."

So after they fed Sage, they wrapped him in a quilt and hitched the horses to the wagon. They stopped at the soddy to tell Papa they had broken the window and needed to replace it. Then they rode into Mingo to the sheriff's office. Lizzie explained what had happened the night before.

When she was finished, the sheriff said, "I don't think you have to worry about him coming back. A man rousted out Doc early this morning, told him his gun had gone off and hit him in the arm. Doc fixed him up, then said he had to tell me about it, because it didn't look like any gun accident to him. The man got on his horse and rode out of here as fast as an antelope. My guess is he's halfway to Denver by now."

The sheriff agreed not to tell anyone what had happened. "It wouldn't serve any purpose to put a scare in your folks, Belle—or in any other lady homesteaders," he said. And then he told Lizzie, "Sister, that was mighty fine shooting. Next time I get up a posse, I just might ask you to join."

## CHAPTER THIRTEEN

# *Becky*

Becky didn't get better. Each day when Frank came to tell them about Becky's condition, Belle hoped for good news, but it didn't come. At night when she knelt beside Lizzie's bed to say her prayers, Belle begged God to heal her sister.

Becky was a sweet, happy child who was kind to everyone. Sage adored her, because she made him laugh. She made them all laugh and forget their troubles. Surely God wouldn't let Becky die, Belle told Lizzie.

As Belle and Lizzie were getting dressed early one morning, they heard a horse outside. The sound made Belle jump, because it was too early for Frank to come by. For a moment, she thought about the man who had tried to break in the week before. She was still frightened he might return, but as the days passed, she had begun to believe the sheriff was right. By now, the man was a long way from Mingo. She glanced at Lizzie, who had heard the horse, too, and looked toward the window. Lizzie had already replaced the pane of broken glass.

*Would Lizzie be scared to stay on her homestead by herself now?* Belle wondered. It would be a shame if Lizzie was frightened off, since she loved the prairie and had never been afraid of being alone before.

"I bet that's Frank," Belle said. "Maybe he came early because he has good news."

Lizzie finished securing her hair on top of her head with hairpins and went to the window. "Yes, I can see Catsup's head," Lizzie said. She took Belle's hand. "We've been through a terrible thing. It doesn't hurt to be careful, but we can't let it spoil our lives."

Lizzie opened the door, then stopped. "It is Frank. And

Carrie." Belle looked out. Frank and Carrie both were astride Catsup. Her sister had a strange look on her face. She slowly slid off the pony, then stopped and held out her arms. Her face was pale, and her eyes were red.

Belle held her breath, hoping against hope that her brother and sister did not bring bad news. Frank had always come alone. "She's all right. Becky's all right, isn't she? I prayed for her. Please, Carrie, tell me she's going to be fine," Belle said.

Carrie slowly shook her head. "Becky died this morning. She was so peaceful. She never even cried. She called out for Mama, and then she was quiet."

Belle ran to her sister and began to sob. Frank tied Catsup to the hitching rail and put his arms around his two sisters. Then Lizzie went to them and embraced the three children, all of them crying.

"She was so little," Frank said at last. "She couldn't eat anything, and there was nothing to do for her. When I touched her, she was as hot as a stove."

"Mama tried. Since we didn't have any sugar left, she boiled the sugar sack to make sugar water, but Becky couldn't even swallow it," Carrie said.

"How is your mother?" Lizzie asked.

Carrie shook her head. "She doesn't say anything, just sits and stares. We washed Becky and laid her out on the bed, and Mama is sitting up with her. Mama won't eat anything, either. I think she wants us to have her share of the food. The little ones are so hungry."

"You're not eating, either, are you, Carrie?" Belle asked. Carrie was as thin as a fence post. Suddenly Belle felt guilty. She and Lizzie had had soup and pie the night before, and she'd even asked for seconds. She should have saved it for her brothers and sisters. She had stuffed herself, while her family was going hungry.

"We came to get you and Sage," Carrie said. "Papa wants me to go into town with him to talk to the preacher about a service. He thought Mama would want Becky buried in sacred ground in the churchyard, but Mama says Becky ought to rest near us, where we can visit her grave. I guess it doesn't matter that the wind will howl over it every day."

*The wind would howl over the church cemetery, too,* Belle thought. Mama was right. Becky would be lonely in the churchyard, with her family so far away. She should be buried on the homestead.

"Becky was a dear little girl," Lizzie said. "You take Sage and go with them. I'll be over later with dinner." She stood beside her soddy and watched as the children tramped through the snow. Carrie held Sage and rode on Catsup, while Frank and Belle walked beside her, carrying the cradle between them. They were a solemn little group.

&#8450;&#8450;&#8450;

Carrie went into town with Papa to talk to the minister while Belle stayed home with Mama and the other children. Belle was shocked at how thin and pale her mother had grown in just the two weeks Belle had been away. She said she was glad to see Belle. She held out her arms for Sage, but she didn't play with him. Instead she seemed to be in a daze. Carrie had once told Belle that Mama had lost a baby born between the two of them. But he was just a day old when he died. He had been born too early and weighed no more than two pounds of butter. *That was different from losing Becky*, Belle thought now. That baby hadn't lived long enough to get a name. Mama hadn't heard him laugh or sing silly songs the way Becky had. She hadn't watched him take his first steps, hadn't made a doll for his Christmas stocking.

"I'll fix you some coffee," Belle said.

Mama shook her head, and Belle realized they must be low on coffee, along with everything else. "I'm glad you're home. Becky missed you. Yesterday she was awake for a few minutes and asked when Bluebelle was coming back. She remembered your full name. I should have sent for you."

Belle squeezed her eyes shut to keep tears from falling. "I'm glad she'll be buried here. I'll plant wildflowers on her grave. Remember how she laughed when she saw them growing on the roof?"

At that, Mama smiled. "We will carry happy memories of her." She set Sage on the floor. "I am too taken up with grief. There is dinner to be got up."

"Lizzie said she'd bring it."

"She is a good neighbor, the best we ever had. She always knows what we need, whether it's food or cheering up. What would we do without her? But still, I must be about my work."

"You sit with Becky, Mama. I'll take care of the little ones."

"Perhaps in a minute. There is something I need to do

first," Mama said.

She went into the bedroom, Belle behind her. Becky lay on the bed. Belle hadn't wanted to see her sister. She was afraid she would remember her dead instead of as the happy little girl she had been. Becky looked peaceful, however. Her skin was white, whiter than normal, but her hair was still pale gold and shiny, just like Belle's. She was silent and still, of course. Belle remembered how Becky had coughed so much that she cried from the hurt of it. She reached out and took Becky's hand and petted it. She had never seen a dead person before and thought the sight of Becky might scare her. Now she was glad she had a chance to see her sister again.

Mama took the scissors out of her sewing basket and cut off one of Becky's golden curls and wrapped it in a handkerchief. "I will send it home to a friend who will make it into a mourning brooch." Belle had seen such jewelry before—watch chains and pins and bracelets made from intricately woven strands of hair. She had never liked it, but now she thought that wearing such a brooch might make Mama feel close to Becky.

Belle stayed beside the bed after Mama went into the

other room. Her face wet with tears, Belle stared at her sister. Then she leaned down and whispered into the little girl's ear, "Bye, Becky. I'll miss you."

*ℓℓℓ*

Papa had gone to Mingo not only to talk to the minister but to buy dynamite. The ground was frozen, and he would have to blast it to open up a space big enough for a coffin. So Papa and Frank worked all afternoon setting charges and digging a grave on a little rise not far from the soddy. They made a coffin for Becky, too. The minister had wanted to hold the service in the church, but Papa said that Mama was not well enough to leave the farm, so the funeral would have to be held beside the grave.

Belle wasn't sure anybody but the family and Lizzie would attend the service. After all, the funeral was to be in just one day, and with the cold, people were staying at home, not visiting neighbors or going into town. They wouldn't even hear about the funeral.

But it seemed people knew when they were needed. And indeed, an hour before the service was to start, they began arriving at the Martin homestead. The Spensers were the first. Mrs. Spenser brought a kettle of stew made with lots of meat for the Martins. She also brought a boiler of coffee for the mourners, because she said people would need to warm themselves. She set a box of tin cups on the table and the coffee on the little stove to heat. Then she took out a lace dress that her granddaughter, Hazel, had left behind and said she would be honored if Becky could be buried in it. Mama smiled, one of the few times she'd smiled since Becky had died. She hadn't wanted her daughter to spend eternity in a worn gingham dress. She and Carrie went into the bedroom and dressed Becky in the frock.

The Rileys came next with all their boys, who looked uncomfortable and stood outside, stamping their feet in the cold. There were children from the school and their parents. Standing a little apart from the others was Hans Kruger, the German man Lizzie had warned Belle about. He looked fearsome, with a heavy beard and sharp black eyes that seemed to see everything. But with so many people around, he couldn't do anyone harm, Belle decided.

Just as they were walking to Becky's gravesite, a rickety wagon pulled up beside the soddy, and the Hansons got down.

Belle exchanged a glance with Carrie, and the two girls moved to their mother. "If she says a word to hurt Mama, I'll tell her to git on back home," Carrie said.

Mrs. Hanson looked around the group, then spotted Mama and went toward her.

"Mrs. Martin," Mrs. Hanson called, and Mama turned around. She looked at Mrs. Hanson as if she didn't know who she was.

"I'm Edna Hanson," the woman said, as if she understood Mama's confusion. "I came—me and my family—for your girl. She was as nice a child as I ever saw. As pretty as an angel. It's a loss not just for you and Mr. Martin and her brothers and sisters, but for the whole community. We all sorrow with you. I don't know why the Lord takes them. I can't help but wonder if He wants the best ones for Himself. It's a hardscrabble life, Mrs. Martin. You've been through the hardest tragedy a woman can bear. But you have your family and neighbors to count on."

Belle and Carrie looked at each other in surprise. That was not what they had expected Mrs. Hanson to say. The two girls smiled as Mama said, "Thank you."

℮℮℮

The service was short because of the cold. People drank the coffee and ate a little of the cakes people had brought. Although many of the homesteaders were as poor as the Martins, they had all contributed something to the funeral— cake, soup, dried-apple pie, corn bread, a jug of buttermilk. But they ate only a little of the food. They knew it was for the Martins, who would be too caught up in their grief to think about meals. Then, because of the chill and because there wasn't room in the soddy for everyone who had crowded in to eat and keep warm, they left.

The Hansons were the last to go. That was because Mrs. Hanson had told one of her boys to milk June, the Martins' cow. "You got enough else to do without the milking," she told Papa.

The Martins and Lizzie stood outside, watching the Hansons' wagon go down the road, then listening to it creak and groan after they could no longer see it.

"I judged her harshly. I was wrong," Mama said. "It is a lesson to me."

"Sometimes people surprise you—for the better," Lizzie

said. Then she added, "It's time for me to go, too."

"No, stay, please," Mama told her. "Stay for supper."

"Your family should be alone."

"You are a part of our family."

Later Belle asked Lizzie, "What did Mrs. Hanson mean when she said it's a hardscrabble life? You said it too, once, the day we met you."

"It means difficult," Lizzie explained. "You have to work hard to make it out here. Life isn't easy. You've already learned that. The land itself is hardscrabble—tough and dry as a board. And it has no mercy. Sometimes things are so rough that you want to give up, but you don't. You keep going, and you know what, Belle? It's worth it. I've learned that. So has your father. And maybe you have, too. I hope Carrie and your mother do one day. Things can be as dark as night, but there is always the yellow light of dawn. I think of the yellow light as a time of hope."

# The Blizzard

They all mourned the loss of Becky. Belle missed the warm little girl who crawled under the quilts with Carrie and her each morning, and Frank missed someone to tease. Papa had a sad look in his eyes when he glanced at the rise where Becky was buried. Sarah and Gully didn't understand what had happened and kept asking when Becky would come home. But Mama missed her most of all.

She tried not to show it, for the sake of the rest of the family. Belle heard her crying, and once she overheard her tell Papa, "Becky is so alone. There is no one to watch over her." Mama's eyes were red, and she wouldn't eat. Belle didn't know if that was because she wasn't hungry or because the meals were skimpy and she wanted her portion to go to the children.

"Mama spends so much time in bed that I need to stay home from school. Someone has to do the cooking and laundry and care for Sage, and Mama isn't strong enough to do it," Carrie told Belle one day.

Belle knew what a sacrifice it would be for Carrie to miss school. "I can alternate days with you," she offered.

"And I'll stay home every third day," Frank added. He didn't like school much anyway.

So the three took turns caring for Mama and the little ones. In the evening over supper, they told the one who had stayed home what they had learned that day in school. So Carrie didn't fall behind at all. In a year, she would still be able to graduate and go off to college. "Mama should be well by then," Carrie told Belle. Neither one of them mentioned their fear that Papa would spend Carrie's college money on seed.

*ele*

The winter was long and cold, but toward the end of March, there were good days. Some of those days were warm enough that the children could play outside without wearing coats.

One morning, the sun was so bright that Sarah asked if she could wear just her sweater to school. Carrie said no, that they never knew when a storm might blow in, so they had to be prepared.

"But it's such a nice day," Sarah argued.

Carrie shook her head, then told Belle, "Lizzie says the spring storms are the worst. They come out of nowhere. So I'm putting the quilts in the buggy just in case." Indeed, Lizzie had told them that she once had started hanging up her washing in the sunshine, and by the time she finished, she could barely see through the snow to her house.

It was Carrie's turn to stay home that day. She said, "If a storm comes up, don't leave the schoolhouse. Papa will come and get you when it's over." Carrie said the same thing each time the children left for school without her. Belle knew she worried about them when she wasn't there to protect them.

Belle wasn't worried that day, however, because the sky was bright blue without a single cloud. Green things had already sprung up on the soddy's roof, and it wouldn't be long until wildflowers bloomed. Maybe she would spot one along the road and pick it for Becky's grave.

She set off for school with Sarah and Gully and Frank,

the top on the buggy down so they could enjoy the sun on their faces. By the time they reached the schoolhouse, however, the sun had disappeared. Still, Belle didn't worry because the sun came and went over the prairie all the time. She helped tie Catsup to the hitching rail, then took Sarah and Gully inside.

The sky turned black just as the children were putting away their dinner pails. Miss Glessner, the teacher, went outside and scanned the sky. She came back in, a frown on her face. "I don't like the looks of this. I think we ought to close school so that you can all go home." There were only a handful of children in school that day, and they lived in Mingo or at homesteads near the schoolhouse. Only the Martin children had a long drive home.

The others rushed out, but Frank and Belle stayed to help Miss Glessner put out the fire in the stove and to make sure the windows were closed. Then they saddled the teacher's horse for her. Miss Glessner looked at the sky again and said, "If you're frightened about going home, you can stay here tonight. I'll stay with you."

"We're not afraid," Frank said.

"I'm not sure it's a good idea to leave," Miss Glessner said.

"Mama would worry if we didn't come home," Belle told her. "It's only two miles. I know we can make it home before the storm gets bad."

She stood on the schoolhouse steps as the teacher rode away and looked up at the black sky. Then she grasped Sarah's and Gully's hands and helped them into the buggy while Frank hitched up Catsup. The buggy top was down, and it took a few minutes to put it up because it was balky. By the time they reached the road, snow had begun to fall.

They drove down the road, into the storm. It quickly swirled around them, and before long, they could barely see. "Should we go back?" Frank asked.

"We can't. The teacher's gone. She's probably home by now. The school's all locked up. Besides, we're . . ." Belle thought about fractions. "A quarter of the way home anyway. We'll be all right." *I hope*, she thought. She didn't admit to Frank that she was frightened.

"Catsup knows the way, even if *we* can't see it," Frank assured her.

Belle knew he was frightened, too. But she didn't want Sarah and Gully to be scared. She tucked quilts around them, grateful that Carrie had put them into the buggy. "I'm glad it's not Christmas. Saint Nicholas wouldn't know which way to go," she told them.

"I don't think Catsup does anymore, either," Frank said. "I'm not sure we're even on the road." The buggy bumped along. "I think the road's over there," he said, yanking on the reins so that the pony turned. "I can get out and look."

"It's too cold."

"I'm tough as a boot." But Frank didn't sound like it.

"You couldn't see anything anyway."

Frank's hands were cold. He hadn't brought his mittens, so Belle took the reins. Although he had a quilt around him, Frank sat with his hands between his knees to warm them. The wind was cold and blowing so hard, they couldn't see more than a few feet in front of them. They went slowly because Belle was afraid they would run into a ditch that was along one side of the road.

"Do you know where we are?" she asked Frank.

"I don't know!" he yelled over the wind. "Maybe halfway."

Fifty percent. *Maybe not even that far*, Belle thought, but she didn't say anything. What did it matter how far they'd come?

"Should I get out and walk next to Catsup?" Frank asked.

Belle studied her brother. His hands were already cold, maybe frostbitten. And he wouldn't be able to see the road— or feel it, either. There was too much snow. "I think we have to trust Catsup." She thought about stopping, waiting until the storm let up. But the snow might fall for hours, days maybe. They would freeze to death waiting for it to clear. Belle thought how awful it would be for Mama and Papa if, after Becky's death, they lost four other children.

Catsup had stopped, and Belle slapped the reins on his back. *He was cold, too*, Belle thought as the pony took a few steps. He stopped suddenly, and the buggy swerved, sliding sideways on the icy dirt road. Belle held on to the reins while Frank reached for Sarah and Gully. The buggy slid halfway around, dragging the pony with it, before it stopped, tilted to one side.

Belle wrapped the two little ones tighter in the quilt. Then she and Frank climbed out. Frank checked Catsup, while Belle inspected the buggy. "The wheel's broken. There's no way the buggy can move," she called over the wind.

"We could unhitch Catsup and send him off, but he might not go home. And even if he did, Papa wouldn't know where we were. Do you think we should walk?"

"Sarah and Gully can't, and how could we carry them? I don't think we could make it even if it was just the two of us. It's too cold, and we can't see. We'd likely wander into somebody's field and freeze. I think we should stay here and hope someone comes along. We can't be the only ones out on the road."

The two got back into the buggy and sat with Sarah and Gully between them. They were all wrapped in quilts. Still, it was cold, and after a while, Gully began to whimper.

"Hush," Belle said, afraid he would start to cry and the tears would chap his cheeks.

Sarah looked tired, and Belle hoped she would not fall asleep. People lost in the snow did that and never woke up. "I know: let's sing," Belle said.

"Sing?" Frank asked.

"We can't dance, so I think singing might keep us warm. And awake." She began a Christmas carol and then a hymn that Sarah liked. Frank sang "Camptown Races," and the others clapped their hands.

They were halfway through "Oh! Susanna" when they heard a dog bark.

"You see, someone *is* out there. Maybe it's Lizzie and

Grover," Belle said. She and Frank began to yell.

"Help us!" Frank called.

"Our buggy broke down!" Belle cried. And then she had a terrible thought. *What if the dog was by itself?* The barking grew closer, although there was no sign of a human. But at least, if they could get the dog into the buggy, it would help keep them warm.

In a minute, a dog the size of a coyote bounded onto the road beside the buggy. *Maybe it is a coyote*, Belle thought. But coyotes didn't bark like that.

The dog put its front paws on the buggy just as a big man loomed out of the snow. "Down, dog!" he called, and the animal backed away.

"We're saved!" Frank said.

Belle was about to reply, when the man came closer. She recognized him—Hans Kruger. *If he is as bad as people believe, we might be better off by ourselves in the snow*, she thought.

# The Rescue

❧

T hat dog, he won't stay still. Then I hear the singing." Mr. Kruger walked around the buggy. "You got a broke wheel, looks like. Well, you don't stay here to freeze. Best you come along to my place."

Belle sunk back into the buggy, trying to think of what to say. She didn't know what Mr. Kruger might do to them, but if they stayed where they were, they were likely to freeze to death. "I don't like him," Belle whispered.

"Me either," Frank replied. "What do we do?"

Before she could answer, Mr. Kruger lifted Sarah and Gully out of the buggy and was making his way through the snow. He turned around and said, "You two, you walk.

I don't carry all of you. Not far. Keep close. You don't want to get lost."

So Belle and Frank, his hands in his pockets, followed the man as he broke a trail through the snow.

Mr. Kruger was right. His house was nearby. Belle could smell the smoke, and then in a minute, they were at the soddy's door. Mr. Kruger kicked it open and went inside, Gully and Sarah still in his arms. Belle and Frank exchanged a look, then followed.

Belle expected a bachelor's quarters—dirty dishes and pots, filthy quilt, rickety bed, dirt clods on the table and chairs. But to her surprise, everything was in order. A wooden bunk was covered by a clean quilt. Another quilt was thrown over a chair. The table was covered by yellow oilcloth, scrubbed so hard that some of the white backing showed through. And best of all, something bubbled in a pot on the stove—a real cookstove, not a two-burner like the Martins had.

On a shelf was a row of wooden dolls. Sarah spotted them at the same time as Belle did. The younger girl reached out her hand for one.

"Oh, you see them, do you?" Mr. Kruger said. He took one down.

"No, Sarah, you must not touch," Belle said.

"Dolls is to play with," Mr. Kruger said, and he handed the doll to Sarah. It was made entirely of wood. Her dress and hat and boots were carved, too. Mr. Kruger took down a boy doll and gave it to Gully.

"Are they German?" Belle asked, staring at the intricate carving. She wondered if Mr. Kruger had made them for his little girl and boy, but she thought it would be rude to ask.

"Yah. I am German, and I make them."

"You carve dolls?" Frank asked.

"In Germany, I am a doll maker. But nobody here wants dolls, so I homestead. You are too big for dolls, so maybe I make you a soldier sometime." He told the children to take off their coats and shawls, mittens and boots and place them near the stove, where they would dry. Then he took out clean quilts and wrapped them around Sarah and Gully.

"We have to get Catsup. We can't leave him there. He's our pony," Frank said.

Mr. Kruger nodded. "You, boy, you stay here. You don't have no mittens." He took a teakettle from the stove and poured water into a bowl, adding a dipper of cold water from a pail. He tested the water, then said, "Not too cold, not too hot. You put your hands in the water. You don't want to get frostbit." Then he turned to the dog. "You stay. Keep the children warm."

"But Catsup," Frank protested.

"Me and your sister will get him," Mr. Kruger said.

Belle didn't want to go back into the cold, but she knew the pony couldn't be left in the snow. She put on her coat and tied a scarf over her head.

Mr. Kruger took her hand and said, "You hold on to me so I don't get lost." He laughed.

Belle went outside with the big man. The snow was worse than ever, and she yelled, "Won't we get lost?"

"Nah, I never been lost." They hurried through the storm until they reached Catsup. Mr. Kruger unhitched him, and holding on to Belle with one hand and the pony with the other, he led them back to the house. "You go inside, keep warm," he told her. "I take care of this Catsup. What a name for a horse!"

Belle heard him laugh as he went off toward the barn.

Inside the house, she removed her wraps, then she asked Frank, "Do you have your pocketknife?"

"If he tries to hurt us, I'll stick it in him." He paused.

"Do you think he'll hurt us?"

"I don't know. He seems nice. I don't understand why he'd rescue us just so he could harm us."

Sarah and Gully were warm now, and they removed the quilts Mr. Kruger had wrapped around them. Bell studied the bed coverings. They were pretty, with bright designs, and the stitches were as fine as Mama's. Mr. Kruger's wife must have made them.

She was rubbing her hand over the tiny pieces of fabric in the quilt when Mr. Kruger came inside. "That horse will be all right." He looked at Belle holding the quilt. "You like my quilt, huh? I make it myself. My wife, she sewed. She sew and I make dolls and furniture." He pointed to a chest with fine carving on it. "Now I do both. And I homestead, too."

"What happened to your wife?" Frank asked.

Mr. Kruger didn't answer. "I heard you sing. Let's sing. I know 'Home on the Range.'"

He started the song, and they all joined in. They sang Christmas carols, Mr. Kruger singing them in German. When he was finished, he said it was time for supper. He handed around spoons, and the children dipped them into a big pot set on the table, because Mr. Kruger had only one bowl. Sarah and Gully were soon sleepy. So Mr. Kruger told them they were to sleep in his bed. "Your big sister sleep there, too. We men sleep on the floor," he said, nudging Frank with his elbow.

Belle tucked the children into bed. Then she wiped the spoons clean. "Mama and Papa don't know where we are," she said. "Maybe Papa's looking for us."

"Not in this storm. Tomorrow it will let up, and I take you home in the wagon. I know where your farm is."

Belle didn't want to go to sleep. Mr. Kruger had been good to them, but still, he might be tricking them. What if he murdered them in their sleep? She vowed she would stay awake all night, but the minute she got into the bed, she fell asleep. She did not awaken until she felt a cold draft and looked up to see Mr. Kruger coming into the soddy.

"No snow. The sun shines," he said. "You will have breakfast, and I will take you home." He mixed up dough for biscuits and baked them in the oven. Then he set the pot with the remains of the last night's supper on the table. Instead of spoons, the children used biscuits to soak up the soup.

"I can help you hitch up the horses," Frank said. "I want to check on Catsup."

"Now I see why you call him that. He is as red as tomatoes. He is fine. We tie him to the back of the wagon. Later I pull your buggy into my barn and fix the wheel."

"You don't have to do that," Belle said.

"I like fixing."

When they had eaten, Belle wrapped up Sarah and Gully. Mr. Kruger picked up the carved dolls and handed one to each of them. "For you to keep."

"They can't accept," Belle protested.

"What good is a doll if there is no little one to play with it? Once there was, but no more. The dolls don't want to stay with an old man." He set the two little children in the wagon bed. Then Belle and Frank climbed up and sat on either side of him on the wagon seat.

With Catsup tied to the back of the wagon, they drove out to the road, past the broken-down buggy, which was tipped halfway over into the ditch and covered with snow. Belle shivered, knowing they would not have made it through the storm if Mr. Kruger hadn't come along. She hoped Papa had not gone looking for them and found the buggy. He would be frantic. But there was no sign that anyone had been on the road after the storm, no tracks of wagons or horses. Papa would think they had remained in the school.

If not for the snow that was melting very fast now, Belle would not have believed they had nearly died in a blizzard just hours before. The sky was clear, the sun on the snow so bright, it hurt her eyes, so hot that she took off her coat. Mr. Kruger's horses were farm animals, and they plodded down the road. Finally she could see their soddy, the smoke coming out of the chimney. Papa was in the wagon, just leaving the barn.

Mr. Kruger called out, "I got your little children," and the children waved as the wagon turned into the homestead. Papa climbed out of the wagon and walked over.

"You brought them from the school?" Papa asked, looking confused.

"They stay at my house. My dog, he find them in the snow. That's one good dog, he is."

Carrie came out of the soddy then and stared. "They didn't stay at the school?"

"It was all right when we started for home," Belle explained. "Then the storm came so fast. We couldn't go back."

"We went off the road. The buggy wheel's busted," Frank put in.

"If it hadn't been for Mr. Kruger's dog, we'd have frozen out there," Belle said.

"He bark, and he bark. He know something wrong," Mr. Kruger said. "He is one smart dog."

"He gave us dolls!" Sarah called.

As Frank took Catsup to the barn, Carrie helped Sarah out of the wagon and took her to the house. "Won't you come in and have coffee with us?" she asked Mr. Kruger.

"Nah, I have work." He picked up Gully and set him down on the doorstep. He turned to the wagon, but Papa took his arm. "You saved my children, Mr. Kruger. I don't know how we can repay you."

Mr. Kruger stopped, and Belle thought she saw a tear run down his cheek. "Yah," he said, looking out across the white fields. "I am glad to do it. Myself, I had two children. One boy. One girl. They freeze in a storm. I did not save them. Their mama die, too. So when there is snow, I keep a watch out for little ones."

He got back into his wagon and turned the horses around and drove to the road. When he reached it, he waved his hand.

"I've heard about him. People say to keep away from him

because he's crazy," Papa said. "I guess I'm the luckiest man in the world. And he's the saddest."

Belle touched the quilt Mr. Kruger had wrapped around her. She would return it to him on a visit. In fact, she vowed to visit him every week. "He could have frozen out there looking for us. I'm not going to believe gossip about people anymore."

# Mama

❧

Mama was in bed when Belle went into the soddy, after Mr. Kruger left.

"Did you tell her we're all right?" Belle asked Carrie.

"I'm not sure she knew you were gone. She took a bad turn yesterday. Poor Papa. He didn't know whether to stay with her or to go to the school for you yesterday. He finally decided the storm was so bad that you hadn't started for home."

"We would have stayed there. Miss Glessner wanted us to, but we were afraid you'd worry, and we thought we could get home before the storm got too bad. She left, and the snow wasn't so bad when we started out," Belle explained.

"By the time we knew it was a blizzard, it was too late to turn back. That Mr. Kruger, he saved our lives."

"Thank goodness!" Carrie put Sage on the floor and hugged her sister. "I couldn't bear losing any of you."

Mama coughed from the other room, and the sisters looked at each other.

"I've been giving her coal oil and honey. The snakeroot is used up."

"I'll ask Lizzie for more. I'll go over there right now," Belle said.

Carrie shook her head. "It won't do any good. Mama has pneumonia. She's . . ." Carrie turned aside, but not before Belle saw tears on her cheeks.

"Is it that bad?"

"I don't know if she'll make it. She really hasn't been well for a year, maybe two years. And she hasn't eaten. Then with Becky's passing . . . Mama took it so hard. She just doesn't have the strength to fight anymore."

"Should we get the doctor?"

Carrie shook her head. "Papa went for him yesterday, just after you left for school. He said there's not much we can do, just keep her warm, let her sleep sitting up, see if she'll drink water. He left some medicine, but it's not any better than the coal oil and honey." Carrie was so tired, she could barely stand up.

"You lie down. Frank can play with Sarah and Gully outside. I'll sit with Mama."

"You don't have to," Carrie said, but she had already spread a quilt on the tarp on the floor. Before long, she was asleep.

Belle tiptoed into the bedroom and sat down on a box beside the bed. In a few minutes, Mama opened her eyes. "Is it Bluebelle?" she asked.

"I'm here, Mama. Do you want a little water?" She picked up a tin cup sitting on the floor and tried to get her mother to drink. But the water only ran down Mama's chin.

"You're safe," Mama said.

"Of course we're safe." Belle thought perhaps Mama really did know they hadn't come home the night before. "Did you see how pretty the snow is? Papa will be glad for it, since it will make the seeds sprout."

Mama didn't reply. She had gone back to sleep.

ℓℓ

For the next few days, Mama was in and out of sleep. The children took turns sitting with her, even Sarah and Gully. Lizzie came over to be with her, too. But Papa was beside her most of the time. "I shouldn't have made you come here, Louisa," Belle heard him say once. "I didn't know I was bringing you here to die."

It was the first time anyone had said Mama was going to die. Now they knew it was just a matter of time. Belle and Carrie cared for Sage and went about their chores silently. Frank stayed in the barn most of the time, caring for the animals. Sarah and Gully seemed to know to be quiet.

Late one afternoon, Papa called them all to Mama's bedside. "I think the end is coming," he told them.

Mama was white, her eyes closed, but her hand moved back and forth on the quilt. "Beck," she muttered.

"I'm here," Papa said. "We're all here."

Suddenly Mama sat up. Her eyes were open, but she didn't look at them. In fact, her eyes weren't focused. "Becky," she cried. And then she fell back on the bed and was still.

"Louisa. Oh, Louisa," Papa said, putting his head down on the quilt. Carrie and Belle and Frank began to cry. Sarah and Gully looked confused.

"What's wrong with Mama?" Gully asked.

Belle reached out for him and drew him to her. "She's gone, Gully. Mama's gone to be with Becky. Now Becky won't be alone."

CHAPTER SEVENTEEN

# Three Walnuts

Things were glum after Mama's death. Only Lizzie's visits brought them comfort.

"How would we go on without Lizzie?" Carrie asked Belle one afternoon several weeks after Mama had died. "She brightens our days."

Those days had been sad for the whole family, and Lizzie was like the yellow light of dawn she had once told Belle about. She showed up two or three times a week with a magazine or a plate of cookies, a book or a bouquet of wildflowers. Once she brought a sack of walnuts. The Martins hadn't had walnuts since they'd left Iowa.

"I wonder if she bought them in Mingo," Carrie said.

*Or maybe that Hank sent them to her, and she didn't want them,* Belle thought.

At first, Carrie decided to use them to make a nut cake. Then she reconsidered. "We don't want to use them all up at once. Let's give them out as treats instead."

Since the dinners the children took to school were sparse—usually lard spread on bread—Carrie decided to give each of them a walnut for dessert. She wouldn't take one for herself, Carrie said, because she was not fond of them.

Belle knew that wasn't true, and she decided she ought to be just as generous. "I don't care about them, either," she said.

"But you used to love walnuts."

"Not anymore." Then Belle added, "Don't put them in the dinner pail. I'll keep them in my pocket as a surprise." So the next day, Belle hid three walnuts in her coat pocket. There was one each for Frank, Sarah, and Gully.

That day was a nice one. The children decided to eat their dinners outside the school. Belle went into the cloakroom for their coats and the dinner pail. Then they went outdoors and sat on rocks in the sunshine. Frank checked on

Catsup to make sure he had enough water. Then he joined his brother and sisters as Belle opened their dinner pail and handed out the sandwiches.

"I wish we had cake," Gully said when he had finished his bread and lard.

"Hush. Carrie makes the best dinner she can. Look at Emma over there. All she has is a cracker."

They turned to stare at a little girl who had gone off by herself to eat because she was embarrassed at her meager dinner. She lived on a homestead that was even more hardscrabble than the Martins' place. Belle wondered what Emma ate for breakfast and supper.

"I still want cake," Gully protested.

"Next year will be better. The harvest will be good, and we can have cake and cookies and pie for dinner," Belle told him.

"I want it now."

"I have something just as good." Belle reached into her coat pocket for a walnut. She handed the first one to Gully.

"Wow!" Gully said. "This is as good as cake."

Belle took out the second walnut and gave it to Sarah.

"We haven't had walnuts for a long time," Frank said as

he waited for Belle to hand him the third one.

She reached into her pocket, but the walnut was not there. She checked her pocket for a hole, but there was none.

"I bet mine is in the buggy," Frank said. "You probably dropped it."

He and Belle went to the buggy and searched. There was no walnut to be found. They looked on the ground around the buggy, but the walnut was gone. Belle checked the other pocket of her coat and even the pocket of her dress, but she found nothing. "I lost it," she told Frank. "I'm sorry."

He looked disappointed, but he said, "That's okay. I'll have one tomorrow."

They went back to Gully and Sarah, who still held the nuts. "We can't get them open," Sarah said.

"I'll show you how," Frank told them. He picked up a rock and cracked the shell, then he helped his sister take out the nutmeats.

He did the same for Gully. The little boy carefully removed the broken shell. Then he handed part of a nutmeat to Frank. "We can share," he said.

Frank shook his head. "I'll wait till tomorrow."

ℓℓℓ

The next day was Belle's turn to stay home from school. Carrie fixed the dinner and packed it in the dinner pail. Then she picked out three walnuts and put them into the pocket of Belle's coat, which she was wearing. "Sage is too young to know what nuts are, but you ought to have one for dinner, too," she told Belle.

"Remember? I don't like them," Belle said.

"Sure you do."

"I like them as much as you do," Belle told her sister. The two girls laughed because they knew they were both lying.

"Maybe Papa will plant a nut tree out here one day, and we'll have so many, we'll be tired of them," Carrie said.

"We'll both be old and married by then."

ℓℓℓ

Belle liked playing with Sage, but she missed the other children, and she was glad when she saw the buggy come down the road. She worked with Frank to unhitch Catsup, then helped Sarah and Gully out of the buggy. Carrie climbed down, books and the dinner pail in her arms.

"Did I miss anything at school?" Belle asked.

"Only fractions."

"Good, because I can't stand fractions," Belle replied.

"You'll have to learn them one day."

"No, I've decided I don't need them. When I go to the store, I'll order a pound of butter and a yard of fabric and a tablespoon of cinnamon. No fractions for me."

"Well, I have one for you. If I put three walnuts into my pocket and take out two, what percentage is that?"

Belle stopped. "Why do you ask that?"

"It's a lesson in fractions."

"No, I mean why did you have only two walnuts when you put in three?"

Carrie made a face. "I guess I lost one. Or maybe I took only two with me."

"I lost one yesterday. I thought I had a hole in my coat pocket, but I didn't."

"I checked for a hole, too," Carrie told her.

"Do you think someone is stealing one?"

"Who would do that?" Carrie asked. She paused,

thinking. "I know several children went outside to use the privy this morning. They had to go through the cloakroom. Maybe one of them took it."

~~~

As she packed the dinner pail the next day, Carrie said, "Maybe I should put the walnuts in here. Instead of your coat pocket."

Belle shook her head. "I think we need to find out who the thief is. I have an idea." She took three walnuts and went to the barn. After a few minutes, she returned, the walnuts wrapped in a piece of cloth in her pocket. Then she climbed into the buggy with Frank, Sarah, and Gully. It was Frank's day to stay home, but Carrie had a cold.

During the morning, Belle watched as several of the students asked to be excused to use the privy. They left and reentered the school through the cloakroom. She studied a little boy, Orville, who took longer than usual to return. He could be mean, and Belle decided to keep her eye on him. When noon came, Belle put on her coat and reached into her pocket. One of the walnuts was missing.

Outside, as the Martin children ate their dinner, Belle watched the other students, especially Orville. At first she didn't notice Emma, who was always by herself, a little ways away from the others. The girl was picking at her hand, then rubbing it on the grass.

Belle got up and went to her. "Did you get something on your hand?" she asked.

Emma glanced up at Belle, frightened.

Belle grabbed for the girl's hand. "Is it tar?" she asked.

The little girl was too scared to answer.

"It came from the walnut you stole, didn't it? I spread tar all over them."

"I was so hungry. I hoped you wouldn't miss the walnut, since you have bread to eat. Are you going to tell Miss Glessner?"

Belle studied the little girl. She was so thin, her bones stood out; her face was hollow. She wore a thin summer dress, and she didn't have a coat, only a square of fabric for a shawl. *Beside her, we seem rich*, Belle thought.

"No, but you must not do it again," Belle said, and then she smiled. "Why don't you eat your dinner with us tomorrow?"

ℓℓℓ

As Carrie was packing the children's dinner the next morning, Belle said, "I'm hungry. Why don't you make an extra sandwich for me?" Then she added, "And maybe I'll have a walnut. I'll take four today."

Carrie turned around and studied her sister. "I guess you found the thief, didn't you?"

# A Surprise Celebration

Belle sat on the ground between the two graves. She had been hunting for cow chips that had been left in a neighbor's field. The man had sold his white-face cattle in the spring and moved on and told the Martins to help themselves. Since wood was scarce, they burned the chips in the little cookstove in the soddy. Cow chips made a hot fire, but they burned fast, so the children were always looking for them.

Belle's burlap bag was full, so she stopped to visit with Mama and Becky on the little rise where they were buried not far from the soddy. It was June. School was long over. Mama had been dead only a couple of months, but already grass was growing over her grave.

It had rained the night before, and Belle could smell the earth where Papa and Frank had plowed the fields. Now she lay back in the buffalo grass, listening to the sound of meadowlarks and watching the prairie hawks wheel in the sky, looking for small creatures in the exposed dirt. A lizard ran across the stones that marked the graves, and a turtle lumbered up the rise. Belle thought she would bring it home to Sarah and Gully.

Almost every day, Belle took wildflowers or pretty rocks she found in the plowed fields to the graves. Sometimes she lay on Mama's grave and cried or wrote on her pad of paper. But more often, she sat in the hot, dry air, looking up at the sky, wondering what it would be like to see the other side of the clouds. Perhaps one day she would go up in a flying machine. She had read about them in the newspapers pasted to the soddy walls, but she had never seen one.

"I bet you can see the tops, Mama," Belle said as she watched the clouds change shapes. They reminded her of giant balls of puff weed. "Maybe you and Becky are sitting on top of them now, looking down at me." She laughed at the idea of her mother and sister spying on her while she dreamed away the day instead of working. "Have you seen a flying machine, Becky?" Belle liked talking to her mother and sister when no one else was around to think she was crazy. She was sure they could hear her and were answering, if only she could hear them.

Then she turned solemn. "Oh, Mama, I miss you. There is a hole in our lives with you and Becky gone. Papa's so lonely without you. And Carrie. She does all your work now, and her own." Belle jumped up then, feeling guilty. "I best get home and help. Our work never seems to be over. The minute the laundry is dry and ironed, Sarah and Gully and Sage get their clothes dirty. We spend hours cooking, and the food gets eaten up so fast, and we have to start over again." She thought a moment. "Well, dinner isn't so hard, because there still isn't much to eat." They were living mostly on pancakes, although Carrie had learned from Lizzie how to cook tumbleweed starts. Belle didn't like them much, but at least they varied their diet.

She heard a wagon in the distance and turned to see Lizzie driving down the road. She had stopped on her way to town to see if the Martins needed anything, and had promised to pick up their mail. Forgetting about the turtle, Belle ran to meet her, and Lizzie stopped the wagon so that Belle could climb aboard. "I got the flour and the salt you needed, and I brought your mail." She held up some envelopes, and Belle could see that one had been torn open.

Lizzie sat for a minute, staring at the open envelope. "I'm dying to tell someone, and it has to be you, because you're the only one who knows about Hank. He's coming to visit. In July."

"Are you going to marry him?"

Lizzie shrugged. "He hasn't asked."

"I bet he's not coming to tell you he's not asking you to marry him."

"I think that's a pretty good bet." Lizzie laughed.

"Will you say yes?" Belle held her breath. She thought back to her earlier conversation with Lizzie, months ago when she and Sage had stayed at Lizzie's house. She'd hoped Hank wouldn't come to Colorado, because she didn't want him to take Lizzie away. That wasn't a very nice thought. In fact, it was selfish. Belle should forget about what *she* wanted and be glad for whatever made Lizzie happy. Still, she hoped Lizzie would turn him down. But Lizzie wanted to be married. And it wasn't likely she would marry one of the Riley boys.

"I don't know," Lizzie said after a time. "I'll have to see what he thinks of Colorado."

"You won't leave, then?"

"I don't want to, at least not until I've proved up my homestead. That's more than a year away."

Lizzie flicked the reins halfheartedly, and the horses started up. "I've tried so hard to make my farm work that I don't want to just walk away. I'm too proud to leave before I own it. Most girls who homestead give up after a winter or two. People thought I would, but I've stuck it out. It's a fine farm, and once I have the title to it, I could sell it for a good price. So even if I marry Hank, unless he agrees to live in Colorado, it probably won't be right away."

"Will he wait?"

"I don't know. I don't know for sure he's going to propose, either. I'll wait until I see him. Then I'll tell you. He's coming here for Independence Day." She slapped the reins on the backs of the horses to hurry them along, then suddenly pulled back on the reins. "You know what I just remembered? You've been here a whole year. I think we should celebrate—just you and Carrie and me. Can you get away tomorrow?"

"I . . . I guess so," Belle said. She would ask Frank to watch the younger children.

"There's something I want to show you girls. I'll fix a picnic and pick you up in the morning."

"Where are we going?"

Lizzie only smiled and put her finger to her lips.

ℓℓℓ

"Where does she want to take us?" Carrie asked.

"I don't know. It seems like it's a secret." Belle was surprised her sister had agreed to leave the homestead the next day, but perhaps she wanted to get away if only for a few hours.

So the two girls were waiting when Lizzie arrived the next day. She drove the wagon. In the back was a basket with a picnic in it. "If we were in Chicago, I would take you to dinner in a fine hotel. Out here, I'm afraid fried chicken and chocolate cake are the best I can do."

"Chocolate cake!" Carrie said, and grinned.

"You can eat all you want. You don't have to sacrifice for the little ones. There is plenty, and they can have what's left over," Lizzie said.

She drove the wagon in the opposite direction from Mingo. The Martins hardly ever went that way, and Carrie and Belle didn't know where they were going. An hour later Lizzie pulled off the dirt road onto a faint wagon trail. After a few minutes, she stopped. "Do you hear anything?" she asked.

Carrie and Belle listened. "It sounds like dogs barking far away," Belle said at last. Was Lizzie taking them to see dogs?

"It does, but that's not what they are." Lizzie slapped the reins over the horses and went up a rise to an open area filled with holes. "It's a prairie dog colony," she said. "The holes are the doorways to their burrows. I think we've scared them away, but let's wait."

After a minute, they saw first one head and then another sticking out of the holes. Then suddenly the little animals swarmed out and sat up, barking at one another.

Carrie clapped her hands. "It's as if they're putting on a show for us." She started to get out of the wagon, but Lizzie warned her to stay where she was. "The prairie dogs are rodents, and they're loaded with fleas. Besides, rattlers love to eat them, so there are liable to be snakes around here."

At the word "snake," Carrie quickly sat down in the

wagon and pulled her skirt around her legs.

They watched the prairie dogs for a long time, until Belle remembered lunch. Lizzie unpacked the food, and they ate until they were stuffed. "We ought to celebrate every year," she said.

"Aren't you glad we came to Colorado, then?" Belle asked her sister.

Carrie smiled. "I am today. And I'm especially glad Lizzie came, too."

# Hank Comes to Mingo

The Fourth of July was the biggest celebration of the year in Mingo, more important even than Christmas. That was because the weather was usually bad at Christmastime. But in July, the days were hot, the roads dry. Of course, there was plenty of work to do in the fields in the summer. Papa and Frank worked in them from "see to can't see," as Papa put it. That meant from sunup to sunset. Belle worked outside, too. She hoed the kitchen garden and picked off the potato bugs, and when she was finished, she helped Frank with the weeding.

By July, everyone was ready for a break.

People looked forward to Independence Day for weeks.

Belle and Carrie talked about what they would wear. Both of them had grown during the year they were on the homestead. Carrie was taller. She had begun wearing Mama's dresses, and she shortened the skirts of her old clothes so that they fit Belle. Belle didn't mind that they were hand-me-downs. To her, they were like new clothes. She chose a calico dress, white with sprigs of blue flowers.

Sarah wasn't big enough to wear Belle's clothes, so Carrie stitched Belle's red sash to the bottom of Sarah's blue gingham to make the skirt longer. Gully had grown only a little, so his clothes still fit. But there wasn't much they could do for Frank, whose pants legs were well above his ankles. Carrie took a dollar from Mama's purse, where they kept their money, and sent off to Sears, Roebuck for a new pair of overalls for Frank. She wanted to buy a pair for Papa, too, but he said no.

Papa had gotten a little shabby since Mama had died. His clothes were worn, and his hair had grown long. Carrie insisted he shave before they went into town for the celebration. She cut his hair, too. And she made him put on a clean shirt. Papa looked in Mama's hand mirror and declared, "I sure am a blazer."

Belle agreed. He was indeed a handsome man.

They offered to take Lizzie to the festivities, but she had to go early to meet Hank's train. Carrie had said he could stay with the Martins, since it wasn't proper for him to sleep at Lizzie's house, but Lizzie replied that he'd get a room at the hotel in Mingo. Belle wondered if that was because their soddy was crowded and noisy and Lizzie wanted him to have a better impression of homestead life.

That day, the Martins piled into the wagon, all except Frank, who was riding Catsup. They stopped to pick up Hans Kruger. He had become their friend, and they always welcomed him when he showed up unexpectedly at dinner-time. Often he brought something he had carved for one of the children, and once he gave Carrie a wooden box. "For the jewels," he had said, and they'd laughed, because she didn't have any. He was a lonely man, and he loved to play with Sarah and Gully and Sage.

Mr. Kruger sat on the wagon seat with Papa, while the others rode in the wagon bed. Frank went on ahead, and in a minute, he disappeared. Belle wished she could have ridden behind him on the pony, because the wagon went so slowly. She was afraid they would miss something.

There was still plenty to see and do, however. Mingo was a drab town, but that day it was all dressed up. Flags hung from the buildings, and there was red-white-and-blue bunting in front of the mercantile. Men wore red and blue shirts, and the women had little flags pinned to their blouses or their big hats. *Carrie should have worn a hat like that,* Belle thought. After all, Carrie was sixteen now, older than the wife of one of the Riley boys and too old to go bareheaded. But of course, there hadn't been money for a hat. So Carrie had worn Mama's black bonnet. Still, she looked pretty and very grown-up.

Papa found a shady place to leave the wagon, and he went off to join a group of men in front of the hardware store. Belle and Carrie took the children to the rodeo ground, where cowboys from some of the ranches around Mingo were taking turns riding bucking broncos. One of the Spenser Ranch cowboys was bucked off, and a man rode in to pick him up before the horse trampled him.

"That's dangerous," Belle told Frank, who was sitting on the corral fence.

"Not if you're careful. That's what I want to do."

"You want to be a bronc rider?"

"A cowboy. Someday I'm going to ask Mr. Spenser for a job."

Frank had never told her that before, and Belle thought it over. Frank took good care of Catsup, and he loved riding the pony. He was a fine rider, too. She was almost as good. Maybe she could be a cowboy—a cowgirl. Belle laughed to herself. There was no such thing. Girls didn't work cattle. But then, people thought girls didn't homestead, either, and look at Lizzie. Belle hadn't thought much about what she'd do when she was grown. Probably get married, perhaps be a teacher, although she wasn't crazy about school. She wasn't crazy about getting married, either, but there weren't many things a girl could do. Belle wondered why that was. Lizzie was as good a farmer as Papa, and Mrs. Spenser seemed to know as much about ranching as her husband, Luke. So why couldn't Belle do something besides teach? Teaching was fine for Carrie, who loved school, but Belle wanted something else. She'd have to think about that.

Frank jumped down and said it was almost time for the boys' race. He and Catsup were going to enter. Belle hadn't known there was such an event. She grabbed Carrie and the other children and ran to a field where boys on horseback were lined up. When they were ready, someone fired a gun, and the race began.

"Come on, Frank!" Belle yelled, while Sarah and Gully jumped up and down. Sage jumped, too, although he didn't understand what the excitement was about. The horses raced off, Catsup in third place. Then he began gaining ground. He passed the second horse and was even with the first when suddenly Frank pulled off to the side and stopped, jumping off Catsup and inspecting his hooves.

"You almost won!" Sarah shouted as they all rushed up to him.

"Something's wrong. I felt it." Frank examined the pony and found his leg was cut open.

"You could have finished," Belle told him.

"But you didn't know that, did you?" Mr. Spenser had come up behind them. Mrs. Spenser followed.

"No, sir," Frank said.

"It takes a wise man to put the well-being of his horse ahead of winning a race."

Frank looked embarrassed.

Mr. Spenser turned to his wife. "You were right when you gave that pony to the boy, Mattie." He told Frank to follow him, and he would take care of Catsup's leg.

When the races were done, there were speeches from a grandstand that was decorated with stars and flags and pictures of President Taft. Belle didn't pay much attention, because she was searching the crowd for Lizzie. She had heard the train whistle before they reached Mingo. So Hank had arrived.

They were singing the national anthem when Belle spotted them. Lizzie looked stylish in a white dress and another big hat, this one the size of a turkey platter, with tiny flags stuck in it. Men turned to look at her as she moved toward the Martins. Some of the men had gone to the saloons and were in what Carrie called a "celebrating" mood. One called out, "Hey, girlie," but Lizzie ignored him.

As pretty as Lizzie was, Belle gave her only a glance. She was looking at the man behind her. She had hoped he would be ugly, but he looked like he had come out of an automobile advertisement in one of the newspaper pages pasted to the soddy walls. He was tall, taller than Papa, and had a small mustache. And in a suit and soft felt hat, he was dressed like a model in the Sears, Roebuck catalog. The men in Mingo were stocky, settled into the earth like tree trunks, but Henry Morrow seemed to walk on air. He was confident, nodding to people he didn't know. When he reached the Martins, he took off his hat. His hair was parted in the center and slicked down with hair oil. Lizzie introduced him, and he told them to call him Hank.

"Lizzie has told me how helpful you've been to her," he told Carrie after the two had shaken hands.

"It's Lizzie who's helped us," Carrie said. "We wouldn't have made it without her kindness."

"She is a good cook and keeps a smart house," he said.

"She's also a mighty fine homesteader. She can plow a field straighter than anybody, and her harvest was one of the best in the county," Belle put in. She wanted Hank to know Lizzie didn't just cook and clean, but that she could hold her own with any man.

"I guess you proved to yourself you could do it," he said, smiling at Lizzie.

Lizzie smiled back, and Belle's heart sank. Lizzie was indeed going to marry him.

The speeches and singing were over, and Lizzie and Hank followed the Martins and Mr. Kruger to their wagon. Carrie took out the picnic supper and handed around tin plates and cutlery. Lizzie had killed two chickens, and Carrie had fried them in lard until they were crispy. There was potato salad and lettuce and tomatoes that had come from Belle's garden. Lizzie had left lemons and a dozen eggs—hen fruit, the homesteaders called them—with Carrie that morning. So there was lemonade and cake. It was the best meal they had had since the Spensers' party the summer before.

"You're a fine cook, Miss Martin. You will make some man a good wife one day," Hank said.

"Carrie's not getting married. She's going to be a teacher," Belle said.

"Women out here sure are independent." He turned to Lizzie. "I guess we can fix that." He grinned at Lizzie, and she smiled back.

*ele*

As soon as it was dark, the fireworks started. The children watched in wonder. Sage was transfixed. He stared at the sky and cried out, "Oh," each time there was a burst of color. Once he put his hands over his ears and laughed. When the fireworks were finished, he called, "More! More!" He stared at the sky, which was made up of stars that seemed to touch the ground. Then he reached his arms to Lizzie. She took him into her lap and held him.

*Lizzie might want to be a homesteader*, Belle thought, *but she wants to have a family, too.* The question was, could she have both?

As they drove home under the dark sky lit only by stars, Hans Kruger asked Papa if Lizzie was going to marry that young man.

"It looks like it," Papa said. "But I don't think he's good enough for her."

"You are right," Mr. Kruger said.

Belle stared at Mr. Kruger for a long time. It was a shame he was so old. He would have made a good husband for Lizzie.

# A Hard Summer

In late July, Papa finally hired a man to dig a well. It took too much time to go to the river for water. Besides, in winter, the water froze in the barrel beside the door. Lizzie said they were welcome to haul water from her well, but Papa didn't like to be obligated. So the Martins used Lizzie's well only when it was necessary. The wheat was coming in just fine, along with the corn and oats, and the harvest promised to be a good one. "The well will pay for itself," Papa said.

Papa had always talked over money decisions with Mama. Now there was nobody he could turn to for advice. Carrie didn't know much about farming. Neither did Belle and Frank. So he asked Lizzie what she thought.

"A well certainly makes sense, but do you have the money?" she asked.

"I can borrow at eight percent interest. It's a good rate."

"The question is, can you afford that? What if the harvest is a poor one, like last year?"

"It's bound to be good. Just look at the crops. And I've learned dryland farming from you and the other neighbors. I know what I'm doing now."

"Why not wait a year?" she said.

"Like you?" Papa asked and grinned. He liked teasing Lizzie.

She glanced down at the ring on her finger. It was a diamond, and Lizzie said they were all the rage with couples who were betrothed. Hank had given it to her on his last night in Mingo. He had proposed, and at last, Lizzie had said yes. He had wanted to be married the next summer and take Lizzie back to Chicago. In fact, he had wanted her to return to Chicago with him right then and give up her farm. Lizzie had said she wanted to prove up her homestead first. "I guess we will figure it out," she had told Belle.

"How come you decided to marry him?" Belle asked.

"Do you remember last winter when you and Sage stayed

with me?" she replied. "That was the happiest time I've had since I've been in Colorado. After you left, I realized how lonely I was. I just don't think I can live by myself for the rest of my life."

The Martin children had liked Hank well enough, but they'd agreed with Papa when he had said Hank wasn't good enough for Lizzie. "A girl like that who likes the wind on her face and the feel of dirt between her fingers, how can she be happy keeping a city house?" Papa had asked.

"Oh, she could get used to it. I think I could," Carrie had said.

But Belle had known what her father meant. How could Lizzie give up the freedom of her own farm just to be somebody's wife?

Now Lizzie and Papa were talking about the well. "I guess I just wouldn't want to borrow, especially before the harvest is in," Lizzie said.

"That's fine for you. You don't have to borrow. You already have money."

"That's right." Lizzie had once told them that she had come west with enough money to see her through five years or more.

"But I have to think about my family's future," Papa said.

"Of course you do. What's more important than your family?" she replied. "But still . . ."

Not more than a week later, a man arrived at the soddy to witch for water. He brought a forked stick and explained to Belle and Frank that he would hold two ends of the stick, and when the third end began to move and point downward, that was where they would drill a well.

He found a likely spot not far from the soddy, and the next day a man came with a rig to drill the well. With Papa and Frank helping, he dug a long way into the earth before he hit water. Then he went even deeper so the Martins would have a good supply in case the underground water level dropped. Then Papa helped the man finish off the well and built a well house around it, with a bucket and a rope to haul up the water. Once the well was finished, the Martins no longer had to drive the wagon to the river for water. And Carrie could use all the water she wanted for scrubbing the house and washing clothes.

"I just wish Papa had put in a board floor, too," she confided to Belle.

So did Belle. "But Papa says the farm comes before the house."

"Men always say that."

They were both happy about bathing in fresh water. Before the well was in, Papa had always taken his bath first, then Carrie, then Belle, and on down the line; all of them using the same tub of water.

Belle had just finished hauling a bucket of water from the well one afternoon when the sky began to darken. Carrie was in the doorway, looking up. "The sky is awful black," she said, frowning. "I guess we're in for a real storm."

"Papa will like that. It's good for the crops. He said it's been too dry."

"It's always too dry here," Carrie said.

The two stood in the doorway until the drops began to fall. Then Belle hurried out to collect the children. Sarah and Gully were playing in the dirt with Sage. She picked up the baby and shooed the other two to the house when something hit her. "Ouch!" she said, thinking for a moment that Frank had tossed a dirt clod at her. Then she felt something pelt her back—twice. She glanced down and saw ice balls hitting the ground. They were the size of small pebbles. Hail!

Carrie ran out and grabbed Sarah's and Gully's hands and rushed them inside. Belle covered Sage's head with her apron as she ran to the soddy with him. Still, the hail hit the boy, and he cried.

They went inside and closed the door, listening to the hail. "It makes too much noise!" Sarah cried. Indeed, the hail sounded like rocks hitting the ground and the sides of the house. The pinging lasted for several minutes. After it stopped, they opened the door. The ground was covered in white.

"Is it snow?" Gully asked.

"It looks like snow," Carrie said as she looked across the prairie, which was covered with white. "It's called hail."

"I don't like it."

"I don't either," Belle said. Then she cried, "Carrie, look at my garden!"

The tomatoes lay on the ground, smashed. The lettuce was shredded. The tops of turnips and carrots were gone, and the vines were stripped of their leaves.

Belle walked carefully to the garden; the hail was hard and cold under her bare feet. "Everything's ruined!" she said. She picked up a bruised tomato and inspected it. They could cut out the damaged spots and still make tomato soup. They could dry some tomatoes, too. She began gathering them and putting them into her apron.

Carrie came up beside her, but she didn't look at the tomatoes. "Oh my goodness!" she said, pointing to the cornfield nearest the soddy. The cornstalks were stripped of their leaves, and the budding ears of corn lay on the ground. "The corn is ruined!"

Belle forgot the tomatoes and stood up beside her sister. "The wheat? Is it gone, too?"

"I don't know. Maybe the hail didn't reach that far."

"I'll find Papa," Belle said, running to the barn. She was in such a hurry that she didn't bother to saddle Catsup. She climbed onto the pony and rode him bareback to the far field where Papa and Frank were working. As she drew near, she saw that the wheat there was fine and green. The hail hadn't extended that far.

Papa saw her coming and walked toward her. "What's wrong?" he asked. "We saw the rain cloud near the house. Did you get caught in the rain?"

Belle jumped off Catsup and stood a moment, trying to catch her breath. She saw Papa staring at her apron, and glanced down to see the red stains from the tomatoes. "Hail," she said quickly. "There was terrible hail. It ruined the corn."

"Hail," he said.

"I never saw the like, Papa. Some of the hail was the size of pigeon eggs. It dented the bucket in the yard and tore off part of the roof over the well." She paused. "The corn's ruined. It stripped the ears right off the stalks."

Papa stared off toward the cornfield, then closed his eyes. Then he dropped his head. "Hail!" he said. When he looked up, Belle saw the despair in his face. "What next?" He looked at Frank. "Come on, son, we better see how bad it is." He hit the fist of one hand in the palm of the other, then led the way toward the cornfield. When he saw the devastation, he stood there, shaking his head. At last he looked at Frank and Belle. "We still have the wheat. And the oats. I don't want you children to worry."

"No, sir," Frank and Belle said together. But they would worry. And they knew Papa would worry most of all.

ℓℓ

It was nearly fall when Belle spotted another strange cloud coming across the prairie. "I don't think it's hail," she said. They had all worried that there would be a second hailstorm. Carrie and Belle never failed to search the sky when they were outside. Papa did, too. They didn't see much of him now except at dinnertime and after dark. He worked harder than ever to make up for the loss of the corn. He had to make sure the other crops did well.

"I've never seen anything like this," Belle said. The cloud moved in a strange way, and it made a whirling sound, as if it were made up of bees.

The two girls stared at the sky until suddenly something hit Belle on the shoulder. It felt like a giant bug. "Ick!" she said, slapping her shoulder. She pulled it away to find a smashed grasshopper in her hand.

"Grasshoppers!" Carrie said as one hit her. Before they knew it, grasshoppers were all over the ground, thousands of them, maybe millions, whirling and gnawing. As the two girls started for the soddy, they saw that the grasshoppers had started on what was left of Belle's garden after the hailstorm. Belle grabbed a hoe and Carrie picked up a rake, and they hit at the insects. But there were too many of them. They ate the remaining tomatoes and their vines, and then they devoured the tops of the turnips and carrots and onions that had grown back. They consumed the lettuce Belle had replanted. Despite the girls' efforts, the garden was gone within minutes. So were the remains of the flowers that Mama had planted the year before.

"They're going into the house!" Carrie screamed. Belle ran after her sister, crunching the insects under her bare feet. They went inside and slammed the door.

"What about Papa and Frank?" Belle asked as she stomped on the grasshoppers that were on the floor, moving back and forth as if she were doing a little dance.

"Maybe the grasshoppers aren't in the fields. Maybe, like the hail, they're only here." Carrie grabbed a broom and began sweeping grasshoppers off the walls. Some were gnawing on the table and on the wooden boxes that served as chairs. Carrie swept them into a dustpan and threw them into the stove. Then she lit a fire.

Belle heard a cry from the bedroom and remembered Gully and Sarah and Sage, who were huddled on the bed, where they had been playing. She rushed in to find the insects chewing on the quilts. Sage was trying to pet them, but Sarah and Gully were frightened and clung to each other. Belle snatched the quilt off the bed, flinging the grasshoppers onto the floor. She stepped on them.

"Thank goodness they can't get through the soddy

walls," Carrie said.

"But they're trying to get in through the door," Belle replied. "They're trying to eat their way through!" She heard the insects attacking the wood.

"We don't dare open it, or they'll come swarming in," Carrie said.

After they had killed the insects that had made it into the soddy, the two girls sat on the bed, holding the little ones, listening to the whirling, crackling sound as the tiny jaws worked away at the door. Belle thought the noise sounded like a prairie fire that Lizzie had described once. Carrie got up and went to look out the window. But it was covered by insects, so she returned to the bedroom.

In a minute, they heard shouts outside, and then the door was flung open. Papa rushed in and slammed the door, but not before a horde of grasshoppers had come in with him.

"They're all over," Papa said. "They're eating the crops. Frank's in the barn with the animals. I came here to see if you're all right."

"We're fine, but they're all over the house," Carrie said. The pests had started chewing her apron, which was hanging behind the door, and she shook them off and stomped on them. Belle scooped the insects off the butter churn, while Sarah and Gully picked them out of the water bucket.

"See how many you can get," Belle told them, and Sarah and Gully began a game of smashing the grasshoppers. But they couldn't get them all, and each time Belle turned around, she saw another one eating the handle of the stirring stick or gnawing on a bonnet.

In a few minutes, Frank came inside, tears running down his cheeks. "They're eating the harness and the handle of the shovel. They're even eating the paint on the wagon. I tried to kill them, but there are too many."

"Yes," Papa said. "There are too many. There is nothing we can do. We will just try to keep them out of the house." He brushed a grasshopper off a wooden box, stomped on it, then sat with his head in his hands, tears seeping out from between his fingers. Belle had never seen him look so dejected. "What have I done?" he muttered over and over again. "What will we do?"

"Why, we'll make the best of it," Carrie told him. *It's what Mama would have said*, thought Belle.

# Carrie's Sacrifice

The grasshoppers left behind a devastated farm. Other homesteaders had suffered, too, but the Martins seemed to have gotten the worst of it. The insects had consumed the wheat, the oats, and what was left of the corn after the hailstorm. And the damage wasn't limited to the crops. The insects had chewed the handles of farm tools. A blanket that had been left outside was in shreds. In the barn, harnesses that were soaked by the horses' sweat had been chewed, and ropes had been eaten through.

The little bodies of the grasshoppers were everywhere—in the well, mixed in with the hay, even embedded in the soddy walls. Belle opened the flour barrel to find a family of them inside. She and Carrie scrubbed the house and the dishes. They burned so many grasshoppers in the stove that the house smelled of them. They washed the family's clothes and aired out the quilts and blankets. But no matter how hard they worked, they still came across the tiny bodies days later.

The hail had missed Lizzie's farm, and the grasshoppers had taken only a little of her crops. Her wheat was all right. "I don't understand it," she said. "My homestead's so close. How can I be spared when you've been hit so hard?" she asked Papa. She had come for supper, bringing with her a pie made from peaches she had bought at the store in Mingo. The Martins hadn't tasted peaches since the party at the Spensers' ranch the previous summer.

Papa shook his head. "I've worked harder than I ever have on this place. I just don't seem to be made for luck," he said.

"Oh, I don't know, Beck. Look around you at these children. I'd say you're a lucky man."

Lizzie always seemed to make him see the good even in bad times. He gave her a little smile. "Why, I guess you've got that right."

ℓℓℓ

Papa was discouraged, and Belle knew he worried about money. "Once we harvest, we'll get enough from the crops that are left to buy food for the winter. But where are we going to get the money to pay off the loan?" he asked Carrie. "And how can we buy seed in the spring?" Now that Mama was gone, Papa tried to talk things over with Carrie, although Carrie didn't have the answers.

Lizzie knew the Martins were in need, and she was generous, bringing Carrie some of her clothes that she said no longer fit. She gave them eggs and chickens, and once she bought two gallons of honey from a farmer and gave them one, saying she didn't know what had gotten into her to purchase so much. Why, the honey would turn to sugar before she could use it up.

Papa was proud, and there was a limit to how much he would accept. Lizzie knew better than to offer money. In fact, Papa refused to accept the two dollars she offered him for doctoring her horse. He said that was what neighbors were for. So Lizzie hired Belle to help her with the laundry and Frank to pitch in with her gardening.

She also paid them a nickel to ride into town on Catsup to pick up her mail. There was usually a letter from Hank Morrow.

"Are you still going to marry him?" Belle asked.

"Why, of course I am," Lizzie replied, although she didn't sound excited. "What makes you think I wouldn't?"

Belle shrugged. "You haven't said much about him."

"No, I guess I haven't," Lizzie replied. "The truth is, I'm having a hard time leaving Colorado. Hank's agreed to wait until I've proved up the homestead. I have to give him credit for that."

"Why doesn't he move here?"

"He's not a farmer, and women here don't have the money to spend on jewelry."

"You could go to Denver and open a jewelry store there."

"Denver's a big city. I might just as well go back to Chicago. Women do not have a lot of choices."

"I don't know if I want to grow up to be a woman, then."

"You don't have much choice about that, either."

&

One afternoon in late October, when the harvest was about finished, the man who'd loaned Papa the money for the well showed up at the homestead. "Well, Martin, I heard you got near busted out."

"Pret' near," Papa said.

"I didn't count on that."

"Do you think I did?"

The man got down off his horse and looked around the farm. He had on a suit and a soft hat, like the one Hank Morrow wore. "I sure am sorry, but that don't change the fact you owe me on that loan."

"And how do you think I'm going to pay it off?" Papa asked. "I'm an honest man, and I stand by my word, but half my crops got ruined last summer. I can't repay you. You'll just have to wait."

"That's not what we agreed on. I got a paper says you'll repay after harvest."

"What harvest?" Papa said. "We didn't have much to harvest."

"That ain't my concern." He looked around. "You got a team of horses over there and a wagon."

Papa almost exploded. "You take those, and how am I going to farm next year? I got a family to feed. You'd leave 'em to starve?"

The man shook his head. "Maybe you should have thought about that before you borrowed my money."

The children were playing in the house, but Belle and Carrie stood in the doorway, listening.

"Your girls over there could work. Hired girls make two dollars a month."

"It'd take the rest of their lives to pay off an eight percent loan. And I'd have to hire someone to take care of my other children. Besides, Carrie there is going to go to teachers college.

"That's a pretty high-class idea. How'll she pay for it?"

"Don't you worry about that."

"My only worry's getting my money back. It's due by the end of the year. If you don't pay, I'll have a talk with the sheriff. Now, as I say, I'm real sorry about that, Martin, but I wasn't the one who asked to borrow money."

The man got back on his horse and rode off. Papa sat down on the stump they used when chopping wood. He put his head in his hands and sat there for a long time. Belle started to go to him, but Carrie held her back. "Don't. You'll hurt his pride," she whispered.

They went inside. Carrie sat down on a box and stared

at the ground. In a minute, she began to cry, tears running down her face.

"Don't cry, Carrie. Papa will figure out something," Belle said.

Carrie only shook her head. "No, he won't," she said. "But I will."

ℓℓℓ

That night, after Frank, Gully, and Sarah were asleep, Papa sat at the kitchen table. He wrote down sums on a used envelope. At last he looked up at Carrie. "I've figured and figured, but I don't see how we can repay that loan."

"Could we go back to Iowa?" Carrie asked.

"And do what? I'm a farmer, Carrie. There's no work for me there. We've got the makings of a good farm here. I took hardscrabble land and made it produce. I can't just up and leave it, but I don't know what to do. I already pawned my watch, but I got only four dollars for it, and that won't take us far."

Belle gasped. Papa's father had left that watch to him. It was solid gold, and it was Papa's prized possession.

Carrie glanced at her sister, then got up and stared into the stove. The lid was off one of the holes, and she looked down into the flames. After a long time, with her back to Papa, she said, "You could use my college money."

Papa looked up, startled. "No, that's yours. Your mama wanted you to go to college. I promised her I wouldn't touch it."

Carrie turned around. "Mama didn't know about the hail and the grasshoppers."

"You're a good daughter, Carrie, but I'll find a way." Papa shook his head. "If I just hadn't borrowed that money! I should have listened to Lizzie."

Carrie sat down on a box beside Papa. "There isn't any other way. If that man takes our horses and wagon, how can we farm? If you lost the farm, where would we go? And it's not just the loan. We didn't have enough to eat last winter, and we're likely to starve this winter, even with the little money you made on the crops. We'll need to buy seed. No, I won't go off to college while the rest of you are homeless."

Papa sighed. Then he stood and went to the door and opened it, staring out at the stars that seemed to be falling down onto the prairie. "I hate to do it, Carrie, but I don't see any other way. There are your brothers and sisters to think about." He turned back. "I'll make it up to you, I promise. Next year, if the harvest is good, I'll send you to college then. And if not next year, then the year after."

"Of course, Papa," Carrie said.

Papa left to check on the animals, and Belle sat down next to her sister.

"I'm sorry, Carrie. It's a great sacrifice for you."

"There isn't any other way. It is more important that the homestead survives than that I go to school."

"Papa means what he says, about next year."

"Of course he does." Then she turned to her sister and put her head on Belle's shoulder. "The problem is, there's never going to be a next year."

CHAPTER TWENTY-TWO

# Mrs. Spenser Comes Calling

Belle's heart ached for Carrie. The family would have fallen apart after Mama died if not for Carrie. She'd cared for the motherless children as if they had been her own, easing their grief and loneliness. She had taken over Mama's chores. She insisted Belle sit outside and write her stories in her tablet on nice afternoons and encouraged Frank to go on long rides on Catsup. And she had lifted Papa's spirits.

For as long as Belle could remember, the only thing Carrie had ever wanted was to go to college, to become a teacher. Now the money that would have given her an education was gone, sacrificed to help her family. Belle felt awful about it. She wished she could do something, but what? It wasn't as if she had any money of her own to give to her sister.

She thought about that one October afternoon as she rode into town on Catsup to get the mail. Carrie had given her money to buy a sack of potatoes. She would buy dried apples, too, if they weren't too expensive. But there would be no dinner in a café or hair ribbons to purchase on this trip. Belle was lucky she had enough money for the potatoes. Although Papa had taken Carrie's college money for the family's use, Carrie kept the purse, and she was even tighter than Mama about spending.

Belle was tying the sack to Catsup's saddle when she saw Mrs. Spenser drive up in her motorcar. Mrs. Spenser was the smartest woman Belle knew. Perhaps she would know how to help Carrie.

"Mrs. Spenser," Belle said, when the woman had shut the automobile door and stepped up onto the boardwalk. Belle stood respectfully, wondering if Mrs. Spenser would remember her.

Mrs. Spenser did. She said, "Why, it's Belle Martin. With the harvest and our cattle roundup, I've been too busy to be neighborly. I hope everyone is well at your house."

"Yes, ma'am."

"Carrie must be excited that she'll finish high school this year. I suppose you'll miss her when she goes off to college."

"That's just it, Mrs. Spenser. She's not going."

Mrs. Spenser frowned and stared at Belle. "Not going. Is she getting married instead?"

"No, ma'am. You see, the money was there. Then the hail and the grasshoppers ruined our crops. She insisted Papa use the money so we won't . . ." She was about to say "starve" but stopped herself. She would shame Papa if she told how bad things were.

"So that's the way of it."

"I thought maybe you . . . I mean, you know all about school. Isn't there something we can do for Carrie? She'd make an awful good teacher."

"Yes, she would." Mrs. Spenser thought a moment. "I could look into it. I know some people." She reached out and squeezed Belle's shoulder. "I can't promise you anything, dear, but let me see what I can do. There are so few girls here with Carrie's ambition. It would be a shame if she just gave up and got married. Well, I mean to say marriage is fine, but I believe your sister might be destined for something else."

"Thank you, Mrs. Spenser. You won't tell anybody what

I said? Papa would be ashamed—"

"No, of course not. Well, maybe Mr. Spenser. We're driving over to Greeley next week. I'm glad you told me, Belle." She paused. "Do *you* want to be a teacher, too?"

"No, I want to write stories. Or maybe be a cowgirl, although Frank says there's no such thing."

"Then maybe you'll be the first."

ℓℓℯ

Belle didn't see Mrs. Spenser for a long time. The woman probably had forgotten about Carrie. After all, what could Mrs. Spenser do? Then, a few weeks later, when Belle and Carrie were hanging up the wash, they saw the Spensers' motorcar turn off the main road and come to a stop near their soddy.

"My, the wash never gets done, does it?" Mrs. Spenser said as she shut the automobile door. Belle and Carrie had been wringing out a quilt, and the woman reached over and helped them spread it over the clothesline. "Did your mother make this?" she asked. "I heard she was a fine quilter."

"Yes, ma'am," Belle said.

"When I first came here to Mingo, I was lonely, and

quilting was one of the things I enjoyed most. Especially on winter days. Working with the colors seemed to brighten things."

"Was it hard back then?" Carrie asked. "Being a homesteader, I mean?"

Mrs. Spenser thought a moment. "We worried about Indian attacks. There wasn't a church or a school. But our homestead was a good one. The best land was homesteaded first, of course. Still, we had bad years." She laughed. "We still do."

"Did you ever think of leaving?" Belle asked.

"When the crops are good, you don't want to leave, and when they're bad, you can't afford to. I'm glad we stayed. It's been the best life I could imagine. You don't like it much, do you, Carrie?"

"It's all right," Carrie replied. But she bit her lip.

"It's important for you to have a chance at something else."

Carrie turned away.

"That's why I'm here. You see, I know people at the Colorado State Normal School in Greeley. I spoke with them last week. They have scholarships, and when I told them what a fine teacher you would make, they said you could attend classes without charge."

Belle gasped and Carrie turned around, her mouth open. She started to speak, but Mrs. Spenser held up her hand.

"You'll need money for living expenses. I spoke with a professor there. He has two young children, and his wife is frail. If you would be willing to help with the children and the housework, you could live with them without charge. He'd pay you five dollars a month. The girl they have now will graduate, so you could start next fall."

Carrie put her hands to her face. "Oh, Mrs. Spenser, I don't know what to say. I never thought . . . How can I thank you?" She burst into tears.

"You can thank your sister here. It was her idea."

Belle shook her head. It hadn't been her idea at all.

"Yes, it was your idea. If you hadn't told me about Carrie, I never would have known she had . . . decided not to go to school. You'll repay us all by working hard and becoming a good teacher."

Belle and Carrie grasped each other's hands, just as Papa came from the barn. "What's this?" he asked.

"Oh, Papa, Mrs. Spenser has gotten me a scholarship to the teachers college in Greeley. I can live with a professor for board and room. Isn't it wonderful! I'm going to go to college after all!"

Papa smiled at Carrie, then turned to Mrs. Spenser. "That's mighty nice. I hated to use her college money. . . ." He stopped and looked at Belle, who stared at the ground. She wondered if he was angry she'd told about the family's difficulties.

Papa put out his hand. "We sure do thank you," he said. "You've been here a long time, Mrs. Spenser. I guess you know how hard it gets. I felt awful bad about Carrie."

"Now we all feel awful good about her," Mrs. Spenser said. She started for the automobile.

"Won't you stay for dinner?" Carrie spoke up. "It's not much, just pancakes, but we'd be honored."

"I love pancakes," Mrs. Spenser said. Then she added, "I believe I have something to contribute." She went to her automobile and took a big can of tomatoes from a grocery box and held it up.

ℓℓℓ

Later on, after Mrs. Spenser was gone, Carrie said, "She didn't mind sitting on a box. And she laughed when Sage spilled his milk on her."

"She's a lady," Papa replied.

"Imagine, she did all that for me."

"I wonder how she knew you needed that scholarship," Papa said.

"She's smart," Belle told him.

"And so is my daughter." He paused and smiled at Belle. "My second daughter."

# Belle Meddles

One night in November, Belle and Carrie sat at the table doing sums on Belle's slate. It had been her day to stay home from school, and Carrie was explaining what the teacher had taught that day.

"Fractions!" Belle sighed. She'd never understand them.

"Don't think of them as abstract," Carrie explained. "There are five potatoes in that dish. So what percentage is each one?"

Belle thought a minute. "Twenty percent. That's easy."

"If we live two miles from the school, and Mr. Kruger is halfway, what percentage is it?"

Belle already knew the answer to that. She'd figured it out

the time they'd driven home in the blizzard. "Fifty percent."

Carrie came up with other questions, and Belle brightened. "You'll be a good teacher, all right."

Carrie didn't say anything. She opened the oven door and took out two loaves of bread, then stared at the black stove. "I'm not going to be a teacher, Belle."

"What!" Belle stared at her sister's back. "Of course you are. Mrs. Spenser worked it all out. Is she going back on her word?"

"No." Carrie shook her head. "Papa needs me. He'll need me just as much next fall. I can't leave. Who would take care of the house? And Sage and Sarah and Gully?"

"But we worked it out fine. You and Frank and I take turns."

"And if I leave, that means the two of you will miss half of your school."

"Fifty percent," Belle said without thinking.

"That's right. Neither one of you could graduate if you missed so much. And that's not all. You couldn't do the cooking and laundry and cleaning and gardening by yourself. And you'd hate being cooped up inside. You're as wild as a rabbit."

"Sarah would help."

"Perhaps. But right now she's too young to do much."

"We'd work it out, Carrie."

Carrie turned around and sat down on the box. Her face was red from the heat of the stove.

"I've thought it over and over, Belle. There's just no other way."

"But it's a year away. Something will come up."

"You know it won't."

Frank came into the house just then. He glanced from one sister to the other.

"Carrie says she's not going to college next year," Belle blurted out.

"I thought it was all set."

Carrie shook her head. "Papa needs my help. But don't say anything to him just yet. I don't want him to be upset. He has too many worries already. Perhaps I can go later, after Sage is in school."

"That's five years. You'd never go after all that time," Frank said.

"Maybe you and Belle can."

"We don't care. You're the one who should go."

Carrie turned her head away—she might have been crying then. She went outside with the dishpan and threw the water on Mama's flower garden, where only a few plants had survived the hail and grasshoppers.

"That's tough," Frank told Belle.

Belle nodded. "If Mama were here . . ." She stopped and thought a moment. "We need Mama."

Frank snorted. "She's dead."

"I mean, we need someone to *be* Mama."

"You mean Papa ought to get married? Mama hasn't been dead even a year."

"I know, but out here on the prairie, that doesn't matter much. Remember Randolph at school? His mother died in a buggy accident, and his father married three months later. Everybody was happy for him. Papa needs somebody. Haven't you seen how lonely he is? Sarah and Gully need a mother. And poor Sage. Every time he sees a woman he says, 'Mama?' " Belle felt awful about her baby brother, who would grow up without a mother.

Frank sat down on the box. "There isn't anybody for Papa to marry. Miss Glessner's too old, and we don't know any spinsters in Mingo."

"No, we need somebody like Lizzie."

Belle and Frank turned to each other at the same time. "Lizzie," they said together.

"But she's going to marry that man in Chicago," Frank said.

"Is she? Maybe she isn't."

"How do you know?"

"I don't. I just know she wants to have a family, but she wants to stay in Colorado. Maybe our family would do. Sarah and Gully and Sage love her."

"But Papa's so old."

Belle thought a minute. "He's thirty-eight. I think Lizzie's about thirty. That means Papa's only—" She stopped and figured for a minute. "Maybe only twenty percent older than she is."

Frank was impressed. "That's not so old. Does Papa want to marry her?"

"Of course, only maybe he doesn't know it yet." Belle grinned at her brother. "That's up to us."

Frank reached over and tapped his fist against Belle's arm. "I guess I better have a talk with him—man-to-man."

Belle giggled at that, and Frank laughed, too. "Well, I

mean I'll talk to him."

"Be careful. He has to think he's come up with the idea on his own."

"What about Lizzie?"

"You leave her to me."

ᘒᘒᘒ

One afternoon, after dinner, Belle rode Catsup to Lizzie's soddy. "I thought I'd come for a visit. I had to get out of the house," she said. "The snow's going to begin before long, and I'll be cooped up inside."

"I'm glad you're here. I'm so tired of keeping myself company that I thought about bringing the chickens back inside." Lizzie was sitting outdoors, stitching on her Crazy Quilt. "I don't think I'll ever finish this."

"Carrie would help you. She loves to sew. Papa said once that watching a lady sew was like looking at a pretty picture."

"Maybe he was looking at somebody who sewed well. It's not much of a picture when your thread breaks or gets knotted up."

"Oh, Papa would still think it was pretty. He's always paying compliments. He's nice that way."

"Yes, your father is a nice man. Do you want a drink of water after that ride?"

Belle sighed. This wasn't going to be easy. "I'll get it."

She went inside and took down the dipper, then went to the water barrel, shutting the door behind her. The door didn't fit right, and it swung open.

"That door!" Lizzie said. "The soddy's settled. I need somebody strong to help me hang the door properly. I've been using a rock to keep it closed."

"Papa could help. He's good at fixing things."

"Oh, I wouldn't ask him. He has too much to do."

"No, really. He'd love to. He says you do so much for us, and we never repay you."

Lizzie glanced up from her sewing. "It would be a help."

Belle turned away so that Lizzie wouldn't see the gleam in her eye. She drank the dipper of water, then climbed on Catsup.

"That was an awful short visit," Lizzie said.

"I just remembered I have something to do. I'll be back."

*ℓℓ*

Later that afternoon, Belle and Papa walked across the fields to Lizzie's homestead.

"Belle says you need help," Papa said.

Lizzie looked flustered, but she also looked pretty, her face rosy from bending over the cookstove, her damp hair in ringlets. "You didn't have to come right away, Beck. It's only a little thing. The door won't hang right. You didn't have to make a special trip."

"It's the little things that get on your nerves," he said, and they both laughed. He had shaved that morning. He'd washed his face and slicked back his hair, too.

Now Papa and Lizzie took the door off the hinges. "It's warped a little," he said. "And the doorframe is out of whack."

"I think the soddy's shifted. They do that."

Papa took off his coat and rolled up his shirtsleeves, showing his muscles. "The frame will need adjusting. Then I'll plane the door."

"I can do that," Lizzie said. She went inside and fetched a plane as Papa laid the door on its side.

"Just along the top," he said.

In a minute, the two of them were working side by side. Papa pried off the doorframe and reset it, while Lizzie dealt with the warped door. They ignored Belle, who had gone off to the barn to feed Lizzie's chickens and milk her cow.

After an hour or more, they were finished. Lizzie said, "You deserve something for your hard work. I have some black tea that a friend sent me. How about a cup of that?"

Papa grinned. "I haven't had anything but sage tea since I came here. But it's awful late. We best be getting home."

"Then come tomorrow," Lizzie said, adding quickly, "you and Belle."

"We'd like that," Papa said. "What do you say to that, Bluebelle?"

"I'd like that, too," she replied, then added, "but I have school tomorrow."

"I guess I'll have to come alone," Papa said.

As they walked home, Papa said, "Do you think that Hank fellow sent her the tea?"

Belle shrugged.

"I never did like him much," Papa said.

"I wish Lizzie would marry somebody else," Belle told him.

ℓℓ

"How did it go?" Frank asked. He was in the barn, milking June while Belle forked hay into the manger for the horses.

"I think Papa likes her, but he hasn't proposed yet." They both laughed.

"Maybe that's because you were there," Frank said. Then he asked, "What about Lizzie?"

Belle thought that over. "I don't know. She likes him, but she likes all of us. Besides, she's engaged."

Frank nodded. "So how do we get her to stop thinking about that Hank and start thinking about Papa?"

"I don't know. Maybe we just leave Papa alone and see what happens."

The two finished their work and walked toward the soddy. When they passed a clump of dried grass that had turned a deep gold color, Belle thought she would pick it and place it on Mama's and Becky's graves. It would just blow away, though. Maybe she'd put it in a tin cup and set it on the table. But there wasn't room for it. *It wouldn't get in the way in Lizzie's house*, she thought suddenly. She remembered a story she'd read in one of the magazine pages pasted to the soddy walls. It was about a man who gave a woman a bouquet of weeds. "Do you know where there's a glass jar?" she asked Frank.

"I guess."

"Tomorrow I'll pick this grass and put it in that jar. Maybe Papa will want to take it to Lizzie."

"Dead grass?"

"She'll like it. Girls are funny that way."

*ele*

The next afternoon Papa washed his face and put on a clean shirt. Belle hadn't gone to school, because it was her day to stay home. Papa didn't say anything about her going to Lizzie's, however.

"I'll be back before suppertime," he said. He started for the door, then noticed the bouquet of weeds on the table. "Maybe I'll take this to Lizzie if it's all right with you. You think she'd like this as much as roses?"

"I would."

So Papa, looking a little embarrassed, took the jar and walked across the fields to Lizzie's homestead.

He stayed for a long time. In fact, it was dark and Belle and Carrie and the children had already eaten their supper when he got home. "I guess I forgot the time," he said. Then he added, "Go look at the night, girls. Lizzie says it looks like there are new stars all over the sky."

Carrie gave her father a curious look, while Belle and Frank exchanged a glance. Papa didn't notice the looks. He hummed a little as he sat down to his supper. Belle hadn't heard him hum since before Mama had died.

CHAPTER TWENTY-FOUR

# Courting Lizzie

❦

It wasn't long before Papa found excuses to go to Lizzie's homestead two or three times a week. He thought her plow might need sharpening or her harness mended. She'd gotten along fine without him for four years, but she didn't say no when Papa offered to help her. And Lizzie came to the Martins' soddy more often, although winter had arrived, and the snow was deep. "I need the exercise, and your house is the nicest place I know to visit," she explained as Carrie made her a cup of sage tea. Carrie and Belle had picked the sage leaves and dried them. Belle thought they had enough to last for their lifetime. She didn't like the taste of sage, but coffee was expensive, and they drank it only on Sundays now.

"Is your father out? I heard somebody on the road and thought maybe he'd gone into Mingo. I should have stopped him. I need some things."

"He's in the barn. But he said he was going tomorrow," Belle said.

"He did?" Carrie asked. "I thought he went last week."

"He has to go again." Belle went out to the barn and told Papa that Lizzie had come for a visit.

Papa smiled and put down the pitchfork.

"She needs some things in town."

"I'll be glad to get them for her."

"I think she wants to ride with you next time you go."

Belle followed Papa into the house. He and Lizzie smiled at each other. She had been playing patty-cake with Sage. "Belle says you need a lift into Mingo."

"Yes, well, I could give you my list, but maybe I'll just ride along. Men aren't so good at picking out yard goods."

"Oh, I'm not bad, as long as it's red."

*℮℮*

The next day Papa brushed his coat and asked Carrie to find

his old muffler for him. "Anybody want to go to town?" he asked. Frank and Belle exchanged a glance, then shook their heads. But Sarah and Gully jumped up and said they would go. Belle thought that might be a good thing. Lizzie wouldn't be marrying just Papa. She would be marrying the whole family.

"You come too, Belle," Papa said. "Lizzie would like that."

So although she had said she wouldn't go, Belle climbed into the wagon with the others, and they rode to Lizzie's house.

Lizzie heard them coming and was waiting on the road when Papa stopped. "Why, it's half the family. What a nice surprise."

Belle started to crawl over the wagon seat into the bed, but Lizzie stopped her. "Let me ride in the back with Sarah and Gully." Before Papa could get down and help her, Lizzie had climbed into the wagon bed.

"It's cold back here," Sarah said.

"That's why we're going to sit very close." Lizzie pulled Sarah and Gully to her and covered the three of them with her shawl and the quilts that Carrie had put into the wagon. "And I'm going to tell you a story about summer that will make you so warm, you'll want to take off your mittens. It's about a little girl who wanted a chip of ice from the ice wagon," she began.

"What's an ice wagon?" Gully asked.

"In big cities, people have iceboxes in their houses. They have compartments for large blocks of ice. The ice keeps the food cold so that it doesn't spoil. A delivery man comes around each week with the ice. He cuts it to fit the compartment. On hot summer days, children gather around him to pick up the ice slivers that fall onto the ground. Chewing that ice is almost as good as eating ice cream. The day I'm telling you about was so hot you could cook pancakes on a rock outside your door."

Lizzie paused, and Sarah said, "That's hot!"

"It sure is," Lizzie said. "This one little girl heard the ice wagon and ran to get a piece of ice, but just as she got there, the ice wagon pulled away. So she followed it to the next stop. But the iceman left again. She followed him all the way down the street, just missing him and getting hotter and hotter each time. By the time she finally caught the iceman, she was lost."

"What happened to her?" Sarah asked.

"What do you think?"

"Did she ever get home?"

"Her mother found her, and I got a switching."

The two children thought that over, until Sarah looked up slyly. "*You* got a switching. That girl was you, Lizzie!"

"Oh, you figured it out."

Papa had been listening to the story, and he laughed. "Out here you can get all the free ice you want."

"Not in the summertime, Beck Martin!"

*♪♪*

"Sarah and Gully sure do like Lizzie," Papa said a few days later.

"We all do. Don't you, Papa?" Belle asked.

"I like everybody," he said.

Belle wondered about Lizzie. She knew Lizzie liked Papa all right, but maybe she didn't love him. After all, there was that Hank.

One morning after a snowfall, Belle tramped to Lizzie's soddy. "It's such a pretty day, I had to get out," she said. "The sun on the snow is so bright, it hurts my eyes."

"Rub a little charcoal from a burnt log under your eyes.

It'll help with the glare," Lizzie advised. She was mixing the ingredients for cookies.

"Papa says you can go snow-blind. He's the smartest man I ever met. Don't you think he's smart, Lizzie?"

"Of course."

"And handsome. He looks like a man in a May Company advertisement I saw in a newspaper we have on the wall. Don't you think he's handsome?"

"I suppose so."

"He's also the nicest man in the world. Don't—"

"Yes, of course he is, but you don't have to sell him to me. I'm going to marry Hank Morrow, remember?"

"Do you have to?"

Lizzie laughed. "I don't have to marry anybody. I said I would because he's swell."

"But don't you like Papa better?"

Lizzie sighed. She reached her arm into the oven to test the heat, then slid a pan of cookies into it.

"Belle, I like your father just fine. I liked your mother, too, but she hasn't been dead a year. And I'm not going to marry a man who's still grieving, even if he wanted to. And your father doesn't appear to be the least interested in finding a wife. He needs a friend, and that's just what I am to him—and he to me. Now, let's talk about something else."

Belle looked disappointed, but she'd already said too much. She thought about telling Lizzie that Carrie wasn't going to college, but that didn't seem right. It was a secret.

"I got an A in fractions," she said.

"That's wonderful."

"Oh, and Papa said to tell you we'd pick you up for the Christmas program at school."

"That reminds me. I want you all to come here for dinner on Christmas Eve. What would you like for dessert?"

"Cherry pie," Belle said. That was Papa's favorite.

Outside Lizzie's soddy, Belle stopped to pick an icicle that was hanging from the roof. She licked it as she made her way across the fields in the snow. The bright sun had melted the trail she had made, and she had to break a new one. Things didn't seem to be progressing between Papa and Lizzie, she thought, rubbing the icicle across her forehead. In spite of the snow, the sun was so hot that she had begun to sweat. Belle was sure the two cared about each other, but that didn't seem to be enough.

# Another Christmas

The Christmas program at the school was held in early December. Miss Glessner had announced she was going home to New York for Christmas, and there wouldn't be any school until January.

After the children performed their skits and readings, there was a dance. A few said it wasn't respectful to have a dance at Christmas, but most people thought it was a good idea. Mr. Kruger played a violin that squeaked too much. Carrie played the school piano. It had been left behind by a busted-out family and was out of tune, but nobody cared. Everyone just wanted to have a good time. Papa danced with Carrie and Belle and even Sarah.

He looked around for Lizzie, but she was already dancing. When she finished, Mr. Spenser claimed her. So Papa asked Mrs. Spenser to dance, and when the music stopped, the two couples changed partners. Mr. Kruger saw them together and played a slow tune.

Since Mama had not cared for dancing, Belle had never seen Papa dance before. She thought he was very good. So was Lizzie, who matched Papa's steps. He swung her around and around, until they were both dizzy and had to stop.

"It's too hot in here," Lizzie said, fanning herself with her hand.

"We'll step outside to cool off," Papa told her.

The two went out, and Carrie started to follow. Belle stopped her.

"People might think it's not proper, their being together outside like that," Carrie said.

"I don't see why. They're always together at our homestead and at Lizzie's," Belle replied.

"Lizzie's engaged, and Papa's married . . ." Carrie stopped.

"Lizzie doesn't have to be engaged, and Papa isn't married anymore," Belle said.

Carrie looked at Belle in astonishment. "Do you think Papa and Lizzie . . . ? Mama hasn't been dead even a year."

"Why does that matter if they're happy? I think it's swell."

Carrie thought a moment. "Maybe it is."

*ꙮ*

"We ought to give Lizzie a Christmas present," Belle said the day after the Christmas performance at the school.

"Her plow could use a new handle," Papa said.

"Oh, Papa, you don't give a girl a plow handle for Christmas." Carrie sighed.

"What should we give her, then? Maybe a doorstop. That door of hers is still awful temperamental."

"Papa!" Carrie said. "A girl doesn't want a doorstop for Christmas, either."

"Ribbons, then?"

"Maybe, if she were ten years old."

Papa threw up his hands. "You decide."

So Belle and Carrie went through the Sears, Roebuck catalog page by page, skipping the pages of underwear and cookstoves and potato planters.

"She might like a dress," Belle said.

"That's not proper. A man can't give a woman a dress. What about a pendant?" Carrie stopped to admire the pendants on gold chains, some with diamonds.

Belle shook her head. "That Hank gives her jewelry, and I bet his jewelry is better than anything we could buy Lizzie."

Finally they decided on a dresser set—a silver mirror with a matching brush and comb.

"It's perfect! All she has is a comb with broken teeth and a brush with half its bristles missing," Belle said.

Carrie took the money from Mama's purse, and Belle rode Catsup into town that very day to send it off to the catalog company. She wanted to make sure the dresser set arrived in time for Christmas. Then the week before Christmas, Belle rode into Mingo each day for the mail in hopes the package would arrive in time. It did.

"What if Lizzie doesn't give anything to Papa?" Carrie said one day.

"I sure hope she does," Belle replied.

*ꞁꞁ*

On Christmas Eve, all of the Martins piled into the sleigh to drive through the snow to Lizzie's house. They would have dinner there, then go to the service at the church.

It was the best dinner they'd had in a long time. Lizzie had roasted two chickens and served them with potatoes and canned green beans. And for dessert, they ate two whole cherry pies.

"A king couldn't live any better," Papa said after Lizzie, Carrie, and Belle had cleared away the dishes and he was drinking coffee. "This tastes like fresh coffee, too. We use our coffee grounds three or four times before we throw them out."

"I wish we could have chicken all the time," Sarah said.

"You can. I'll give you some baby chicks in the spring. You can raise them, Sarah," Lizzie told her.

"We don't have a chicken coop."

"Your papa could build one, I bet. He's awful good at building things." Lizzie and Papa exchanged a look.

As everyone left the soddy to climb into the sleigh for church, Belle said she had left her mittens inside. She slid a package from the sleigh under her shawl and went back in. She laid it on the table. *It's not wrapped,* she thought, *but then who has fancy Christmas paper?* But there was a card. Belle and Carrie had spent a great deal of time discussing what should be written on it. Belle thought it ought to say something such as "This is so you can see how pretty you are." Carrie said that was gushy and something their father would never write. But she couldn't come up with anything better. So at last, they signed the card, *Beck Martin.*

℘

On Christmas morning, it snowed so hard, the Martins couldn't see as far as their barn. When he went to milk June, Frank had to hold on to the rope Papa had tied between the soddy and the barn. That way, he wouldn't get lost if there was a bad storm. Carrie and Belle had baked bread the day before, so they had milk toast for breakfast. The younger children played with the carved horses Mr. Kruger had given them. He said Saint Nick had left them at his house by mistake. Lizzie had given them presents the night before. Papa opened his and grinned at the bright red muffler.

"What did we give her?" Papa asked.

"A lace collar. I crocheted it from the string I saved from our packages at the mercantile," Carrie said.

"I'm sure she'll like it. Lizzie likes everything."

"Including you," Belle mouthed, but Papa didn't see her.

The storm lasted two days. When it was over, Papa said, "I'd better check on our neighbor to make sure everything is all right after the blizzard."

"You mean Mr. Kruger?" Belle asked with a straight face.

"Who else?" Papa said, wrapping the red muffler around his neck. "Oh, maybe I should check on Lizzie, too."

"That's not a bad idea," Belle said.

"I may be gone awhile. The snow's awful deep," Papa said as he left the soddy. He didn't return until suppertime. His face was red from the cold, and he was whistling.

"How are our neighbors?" Carrie asked.

"They're fine. Hans was working on a quilt."

"And Lizzie?"

Papa sat down on a box and looked at his two older daughters. "It seems an odd thing happened Christmas Eve. Somebody left a package with a silver mirror and a brush and a comb on Lizzie's table and signed my name to it.

Would you know anything about that?"

Belle and Carrie exchanged a glance, but neither one answered.

"I told her it wasn't from me, but she wouldn't believe me." He shook his head and smiled to himself.

# *Papa's Surprise*

One day in early February Mrs. Hanson visited the Martins' soddy. "I was just driving past and thought I'd stop and be neighborly," she said. She reached out her hand so that Papa could help her down from her wagon.

"I'll fix you a cup of sage tea," Belle said. She wasn't about to use their precious coffee for Mrs. Hanson. They all appreciated how kind she had been at Mama's funeral the year before, but still, she had a sharp tongue and was the worst gossip in Bondurant County. Some people were both good and bad, Belle decided.

"The weather's been so poor, I haven't gotten out, so I haven't a word of news," she said.

*You mean gossip*, Belle thought.

"Well, we don't have any, either," Carrie told her.

"Hans Kruger got a new fiddle. I picked it up for him when I went for the mail," Papa said.

"He's got as sociable as a tomcat," Mrs. Hanson said. "I don't know if I like that. There are stories about him. . . ."

"He saved my children. He's as good a neighbor as we have," Papa said.

"Just the same . . ." Mrs. Hanson held out her cup for more tea. "I guess you take pretty good care of him." She eyed Papa. "Him and Lizzie Cord."

"We hope to take care of all our neighbors, and they take care of us," Carrie said quickly.

"Especially Lizzie," Mrs. Hanson said. "There's talk about it, I can tell you, her and you, Mr. Martin. It don't look good. No, it don't. She's an engaged woman, and your poor wife ain't been dead quite a year."

"I guess it's nobody's business," Papa said.

"You know how folks are. When they tell me, I say it's a pretty sharp move on your part, you losing all your crops last year and her having money." Mrs. Hanson shook her head back and forth. "Folks are saying Beck Martin is a mighty smart man that way."

Belle had poured more tea into Mrs. Hanson's cup, but instead of handing it to her, she set it on the stove. Carrie stood up, making it clear that it was time for their guest to leave.

Mrs. Hanson understood. "Excuse me if I said too much, but you ought to know what people think. I've never been afraid to tell it straight to folks."

"No, we've heard that about you," Carrie said. She rarely was rude, and Belle looked at her sister in surprise.

"I'm not the one saying it."

"You just did," Belle told her.

Papa hadn't said anything, but now he spoke. "You embarrassed my children, Mrs. Hanson."

"It's you who embarrassed them, Mr. Martin, courting a woman for her money."

She went outside and climbed into her wagon. Papa handed her the reins. They all watched her drive out to the road and then turn toward Lizzie's place.

"We ought to warn Lizzie," Belle said.

"Warn her of what, that her neighbor is after her money?" Papa said. "I hadn't realized we were the talk of the county."

He turned and walked to the barn.

"Mrs. Hanson was cruel. Papa doesn't care about Lizzie's money," Carrie said.

"He just wants Lizzie," Belle replied. "At least I think he does."

ℒℓℯ

Papa stayed on the homestead after that, not venturing out to visit neighbors or even go to town. And Lizzie didn't come to visit. Belle blamed Mrs. Hanson for it.

"He's not going to marry her, is he?" Frank asked Belle one day as they watched Papa stare into the distance.

"I don't know."

"Next time I see Billy Hanson, I'm going to beat him up. I'll tell him to give that to his mother."

Belle rode Catsup to Lizzie's soddy twice, but Lizzie wasn't home either time. Belle worried that Mrs. Hanson's meddling had made a mess of things. Not only was Papa not going to get married, they'd lost the friendship of the neighbor they loved so much.

Papa spent much of his time in the barn now, preparing

for spring planting. When he was in the house, he was silent. Sometimes Papa just took off walking and didn't come home until suppertime. Once Belle saw him standing among the yucca beside Mama's grave, talking to her. He was there a long time and when he left, he had tears on his face.

In late February, Belle rode into Mingo for the mail. She asked for Lizzie's mail, too. That would be a good excuse to stop at Lizzie's once more.

"Miss Cord said she'd pick it up when she got back," the postmaster said.

"Lizzie's gone?"

"Chicago. She left a few days ago. Didn't say when she'd return. Hans Kruger is looking after her dog. If you ask me, I'd say Miss Cord's gone to marry that fellow who came to see her last summer. He seemed mighty nice."

"He isn't," Belle said.

"He's not?" The postmaster looked at her curiously.

"I mean he is, but he's not good enough for her."

"That's what you women always say."

Belle went home with a heavy heart.

"Lizzie went to Chicago," she announced at dinner. "Nobody knows when she's coming back—*if* she's coming back."

Carrie and Frank were stunned, but Papa just kept on eating. "I guess that's her business."

"The postmaster said he thought she was going to marry that Hank."

They all turned to Papa, but he didn't look up. "Not our business," he repeated.

"But, Papa—" Belle started.

Papa cut her off. "I don't want to hear anything more about Lizzie getting married. There's been too much meddling already."

Belle turned red. Papa was talking about her, of course. Suddenly she wasn't hungry. She stood and went outside and began to cry. Everything was a muddle, and it was all her fault. Maybe if she had kept out of it, Papa and Lizzie would have fallen in love on their own. In a minute, she felt a hand on her shoulder and turned to see Papa. "The wind blew something into my eyes," she said, because she didn't want him to know she'd been crying.

"Little Bluebelle," he said, not unkindly. "You always have the best intentions."

"Do you think she'll come back?" Belle asked. "After all,

it's almost time for planting. Lizzie wouldn't just leave her homestead, would she?"

Papa smiled then, and Belle thought what a kind father he was. "We'll just have to wait and see."

*ଯ୍ଯୋ*

March came and the weather turned fine. On one particularly sunny day, Papa announced he was going into town to pick up seed.

"I'll go with you," Belle said. She loved the quiet ride down the dirt road in the early spring with the meadowlarks singing and the smell of newly turned earth. Maybe Papa would open up about what had happened between Lizzie and him. He'd barely mentioned Lizzie's name after Mrs. Hanson's visit.

"Not this time, Bluebelle. I have some heavy thinking to do," he said. "I do it best alone. You can ride along with me next time."

Belle was disappointed. She watched her father climb into the wagon, thinking how handsome he looked, his hair combed, his face washed, and wearing a clean shirt that was only a little patched. Lizzie didn't know what she was missing.

"It's such a nice day that we ought to wash the quilts," Carrie announced as Belle watched the wagon get smaller and smaller on the road. Carrie got out the big copper boiler, filled it with water, and set it on the stove. When the water was hot, the two girls carried the boiler outside and began washing the quilts with the lye soap they had made in the fall. Meanwhile, Frank cleaned out a big container from the barn and filled it with cold water. Carrie told him to put in a little pepper, which would help remove the soap from the quilts.

Carrie and Belle took turns rubbing the first quilt up and down on the scrub board. When it was clean, they wrung it out. Frank, with the help of Sarah and Gully and even Sage, dipped the quilt into the clear water, then spread it over the clothesline. Carrie and Belle heated more water in the boiler and washed a second quilt, and then a third. As the younger children spread the third quilt over the clothesline, the line began to sag, and Frank yelled for help.

"The wet quilts are too heavy," he cried.

Belle and Carrie reached the clothesline in time to keep

the quilts from falling into the dirt. While Frank held up the line, Belle and Carrie removed the last quilt. Gully and Sarah brought the apple-box seats from the house, and they spread the third quilt over them.

"I guess that's all the laundry for today," Carrie announced. She looked around at her family. "I know; since we don't have anything to sit on in the house, let's have a picnic outside. We'll eat dinner in the yard."

Dinner wasn't much different from what they usually ate in the soddy, but eating outside was fun. They sat on rocks and ate their pancakes. Then Carrie announced a game. "We'll play an alphabet game. Who can see something that starts with the letter 'A'?"

"'Apple,'" Frank announced, pointing to a picture on one of the crates they used for stools.

"'B,'" Carrie said.

There were lots of "B" words outside—"branch," "bedding." Frank started to say one, but Belle shook her head, then nodded at Sarah and Gully.

"I know. 'Belle,'" Gully said, pointing at his sister.

"'C.'"

"'Carrie!'" Sarah yelled.

"'D.'"

Then they went down the alphabet until they came to "L."

"'Lizzie,'" Sarah said.

"It has to be something you can see. Lizzie's not here," Belle told her.

"Yes, she is too!" Sarah pointed to the road.

They had been too caught up in the game to pay attention to the wagon coming down the dirt road. Now they looked up to see Papa turning into the homestead. Lizzie sat on the seat beside him.

"Lizzie!" Belle called. She looked hard at the wagon bed to see if Hank was there. She wondered if Lizzie and Hank had gotten married and Papa had gone into town to pick them up. Maybe Lizzie had come home to stay until she proved up her land. Or perhaps she was just packing up her things before returning to Chicago. Belle turned away, her eyes filled with tears, sure that she was right. She didn't want to congratulate Lizzie. But that was thoughtless. *Lizzie is my friend,* thought Belle. *I should be happy for her, even if I am sad for Papa.*

The others gathered around the wagon, and finally Belle joined them.

"We missed you, Lizzie. We thought you got married," Carrie said.

"Not yet, but I'm going to."

"In Chicago?" Carrie asked.

"No. Right here in Mingo. I did go to Chicago, though. I had to tell Hank in person that I wasn't going to marry him. I had to give him back his ring, too."

They all looked confused, except for Belle, whose eyes lit up. She grinned at Lizzie and Papa. "Who are you going to marry, then?"

"You want to tell them?" Lizzie asked Papa.

He had taken a gold watch out of his pocket. Belle recognized it as the one he had sold. She knew suddenly that Lizzie had found it and given it to him. "We best hurry if we don't want to be late for the wedding," Papa said.

"But who are you going to marry, Lizzie?" Sarah asked.

Lizzie took Papa's hand and smiled up at him. "Some fellow named Beck Martin. Now, everybody, get into the wagon. We can't have a wedding without the family." She looked at the children gathered around them and added, "Our family."

# Epilogue

Papa and Lizzie built a house that straddled the property line between their two farms. That way, they could establish that each had lived on the land long enough to acquire title to the two homesteads. The crops did well over the years, and when Hans Kruger died, Papa purchased his homestead. Later on, he bought out the Hansons, so that eventually, he and Lizzie had a large, prosperous farm.

All of the Martin children graduated from college, including the three who were born to Lizzie and Papa. Both Carrie and Sarah became teachers. Carrie, in fact, became a county superintendent of schools in Iowa. Frank worked as an executive for a sugar beet company, but his heart always was in ranching. He saved his money, and after Luke and Mattie Spenser died, he bought their ranch. Gully became a lawyer in Denver, while Sage studied at the agricultural college in Fort Collins. He then returned to Mingo to help manage the Martin farm.

Papa and Lizzie were proud of all their children, but they just might have been proudest of Belle. She became a writer, and one day she published a book about growing up on a homestead in eastern Colorado. She dedicated it to "My two mamas, Louisa and Lizzie, fifty percent to each."

# Glossary

**Bed tick:** A large bag stuffed with hay, dried grass, or feathers to form a mattress. The tick is often made out of blue-and-white-striped fabric called mattress ticking.

**Blazer:** A fine-looking person

**Buffalo grass:** A type of short, dry grass common on the prairie

**Bugged up:** Dressed up

**Bunting:** Long strips of cheap cotton cloth used for decoration. Bunting often comes in red, white, and blue for Fourth of July.

**Cow chips:** Circles of cow dung. When dry, they are used as fuel by homesteaders.

**Dinger:** Something special, short for humdinger

***Driving costume:*** An outfit usually made up of a long coat, a hat, gloves, and goggles, worn to keep clean when riding in an open car on a dusty road.

***Dryland farming:*** Raising crops on land with little water

***Evaporated milk:*** Concentrated, unsweetened milk sold in cans and used when fresh milk is not available

***Fatback:*** A strip of pork fat

***Flatiron:*** A heavy iron used to press clothes. The iron is heated by leaving it facedown on a hot stove.

***Foodstuffs:*** Anything suitable for food

***Lard pail:*** A metal container with bail handle containing store-bought lard. The buckets are often reused as lunch boxes.

***Oilcloth:*** A fabric treated with oil to make it waterproof. Printed with colorful designs, it is used for tablecloths or to line shelves.

***Ragged out:*** Dressed up

**Reo:** An automobile made by the Reo Motor Car Company

**Shirtwaist:** A tailored blouse

**Snakeroot:** A plant whose roots supposedly cure snakebites and various illnesses

**Starter:** A mixture of flour, water, and active yeast. When a person mixes bread dough, she/he uses the starter instead of yeast. She/he pinches off a piece of the dough to save as a starter for the next batch of bread.

**Stove black:** A mixture of pigment and wax rubbed onto a stove to keep it black

**Touring car:** A large automobile that seats several people and is suitable for long drives

**Tumbleweed starts:** Russian thistle shoots

**Witch:** Using a forked stick to locate underground water. When the end of the stick moves downward, it is supposed to indicate water. Witching for water is common in pioneer times, although there is no scientific evidence that it works.

# Acknowledgments

Twice a year when I was growing up, my family made the long drive from our home in Denver to my grandparents' farm in Harveyville, Kansas. In those days before car radios, we sang, played games, and waved to long-haul truck drivers and locomotive engineers. And we studied the farms along the two-lane highway. Because I loved stories, I wondered about the people who had settled those farms—who they were, why they came west, and whether they stayed or gave up and moved on.

Many of the early farmers were homesteaders—families who had come west to claim free land. In 1862, the U.S. Congress passed the Homestead Act. It allowed adults, including women and immigrants, to apply for 160 acres of government land, most of it west of the Mississippi River. After living on the land for five years, the homesteader was given title to it. In 1909, the amount of land was doubled to 320 acres. Over the years, 1.6 million homesteaders claimed 270 million acres, or 10 percent of the United States.

Many of those homesteaders were successful and developed prosperous farms. They established towns and built schools and churches. Still, farming was hard work, and much of the land was unsuitable for crops. The farms were isolated, and people suffered from loneliness. So some of the families gave up. On those trips to Kansas, I saw their deserted houses—soddies melting into the ground and frame houses with the paint peeling off, the windows gone. I couldn't help wondering who the homesteaders were and what their lives had been like. So when Jack Martin, the husband of my childhood friend Diane Terry, gave me a booklet with stories about early settlers, I decided to write *Hardscrabble.*

Thank you, Jack and Diane. Thank you, Barb McNally, for your perceptive editing, and Robert Marcell at the Homestead National Monument of America for your help with homestead laws. As always, thank you, Danielle Egan-Miller, for your support and friendship. My thanks and love to my own family—Bob, Dana, Kendal, Lloyd, and Forrest.

# Sandra Dallas

Sandra Dallas is the *New York Times*–bestselling author of *The Quilt Walk* and *Red Berries, White Clouds, Blue Sky.* She has written ten nonfiction books and fourteen adult novels, including *The Last Midwife, Prayers for Sale, The Diary of Mattie Spenser,* and *The Persian Pickle Club.* A former Denver bureau chief for *Business Week* magazine, she is the recipient of two National Cowboy & Western Heritage Museum Wrangler Awards, three Western Writers of America Spur Awards, and four Women Writing the West WILLA Awards. She lives in Denver. Visit her at www.sandradallas.com.